MW0081 7874

"There's nothing loose about
from the beginning, and he ot.___ ___ ____ __
the young voice of the eighties and nineties Chicanos who
will keep this segment of American literature lively and
vibrant. Welcome, then, to the voice and to the world of
David Rice."
—Rolando Hinojosa, author of *The Valley*

"Fourteen stories . . . deliver clever irony in the somewhat
shocking discoveries made while moving from child to
adult . . . . each a perfectly formed gem . . ."
—*Hispanic*

". . . his Edcouch comes alive as a setting, and it'll be interesting to see where the author's future work takes him."
—*Kirkus Reviews*

Bilingual Press/Editorial Bilingüe

GIVE THE PIG *a*
CHANCE
& Other Stories

David Rice

Bilingual Press/Editorial Bilingüe
TEMPE, ARIZONA

© 1996 by Bilingual Press/Editorial Bilingüe

ISBN 0-927534-54-1

Library of Congress Cataloging-in-Publication Data

Rice, David, 1964-
    Give the pig a chance & other stories / by David Rice.
        p.   cm.
    ISBN 0-927534-54-1 (paper : alk. paper)
    1. Mexican American Border Region—Social life and customs—
Fiction.   2. Rio Grande Valley—Social life and customs—Fiction.
3. Mexican Americans—Rio Grande Valley—Fiction.   4. Texas—Social
life and customs—Fiction.   5. Mexican Americans—Texas—Fiction.
I. Title.
PS3568.I273G58   1995
813'.54—dc20   95-31048
                                                    CIP

PRINTED IN THE UNITED STATES OF AMERICA
Second printing, December 1998

Front and back cover photographs by Christopher Caselli
Cover design by Laura Cloud

Acknowledgments

Partial funding provided by the Arizona Commission on the Arts through appropriations from the Arizona State Legislature.

The author expresses his appreciation to Dr. Jaime Mejía, Dr. Martha L. Brunson, and Beverley Braud of the Department of English at Southwest Texas State University.

CONTENTS

For Carol

and

to the memory of my brother

The Circumstances
Surrounding My Penis

Up to the age of eight, I thought I was pretty normal. I was a healthy kid with too much energy. Running around and playing with my friends and fighting with my brother. I couldn't complain much until my cousin's neighbor, Lolita, informed me that I wasn't normal because I had a "funny-looking" penis.

My cousins Arnie and Berto were three and four years older than I, respectively. They lived with Mama Locha, my grandmother, in Weslaco, Texas, about ten miles south of Edcouch. It was a bigger town than Edcouch, but most of the houses this side of the railroad tracks were no better than the houses in Edcouch. Mama Locha's house had indoor plumbing like many houses in that part of town, but it also had an outhouse.

It was a small outhouse, divided in half. One half was the toilet and the other half was the shower. Each had a door that locked with a latch. Both the toilet and the shower worked just fine, but they were a little scary to use at night because there was no light, and I had this fear of a spider or a snake or something, anything, biting my butt.

Lolita was Berto's age, and whenever my cousins wanted to play doctor or house, she was the perfect nurse or wife. She liked to do "mañas," and most of the boys in the neighborhood knew it. She was cute and actually real nice. She had this look in her eyes. The kind of look a woman gives you when she begins putting you into a hypnotic trance. Now that I'm older I realize that hypnotic eyes are very rare, but at eleven Lolita was a master.

Lolita's eyes could make you do anything. All she had to do was turn them on and you agreed to whatever she asked. And she wanted to look at my pipi. I know that there are other names: tally whacker, dingy whopper, thingy, and of course the name that works for both boys and girls, "down there." When she told me she wanted to see my pipi I was really blown away. But what really knocked me out was that she followed her request with a deal: "If you show me yours, I'll show you mine."

After a few seconds I said yes, but I told her she had to show me hers first.

She nodded okay in one quick second; Lolita was a pro. It was as if she did this sort of thing all the time. I asked where could we go to do this and she said, "The outhouse." She told me to go into the shower half first, and she would wait to make sure no one was watching, then she would go in.

As I waited in the outhouse, I tried to imagine what it would look like. I had seen baby girls getting their diapers changed, but I knew that it couldn't still look like that once they got older. I heard her light footsteps approaching, and I stood to one side to give her room.

Lolita looked at me, and I said we had to hurry before someone tried to use the outhouse. My eyes focused on her hands as she unbuttoned her pants. She wiggled her body slightly and pulled her pants and panties down to her thighs at the same time. It still looked like what baby girls had! There was just this vertical line and nothing else?

"Okay, your turn," she said, pulling her pants and panties back up. I unbuttoned my jeans and unzipped the zipper, bringing my jeans and Fruit-of-the-Loom underwear down together. I looked to see what her reaction would be. I was hoping she would be amazed and say "wow" or "eeelooooo" or anything that would make her want to look at it more closely.

But instead Lolita had a puzzled look on her face. "Why does it look like that? It's funny-looking. Why is it so small? The pipis of Arnie and Berto don't look like that." I had no answers for Lolita. I lowered my eyes and looked at the drain surrounded by the cool, dark cement. I began to pull my pants back on as she slipped out the door. I didn't see or talk to Lolita the rest of the day, and I didn't tell any of my friends about what I did in the outhouse.

After a few weeks I managed to put aside what Lolita had said about my penis, and I didn't see her that often anyway. When I did see her, she didn't offer to play doctor or house with me, but there were always other things to do at Mama Locha's.

A couple of years went by. I was in the fifth grade, and no one had seen my pipi since that day in the outhouse. I was in the boy's room ready to pee and kept my eyes on the metal pipe above the trough that delivered the water. Looking at the pipe where I knew water flowed somehow made me pee a lot more easily. I heard someone come in, but I didn't turn around and just kept my eyes on the pipe.

Out of the corner of my eye I could see it was Fide Flores Fuentes, a kid in my class. He stood next to me and began to pee as well. I could hear him pee, but I kept my eyes on the pipe. I could feel that he was looking at me.

"Hey, what's wrong with it?" he said, motioning with his head and eyes at my penis.

I gave him a confused look. "¿Qué?"

"Your thing. Why does it look like that? It's got that red ring around it," Fide Flores said.

I knew what he was talking about. My penis had a thin, pink circle around the top, but I didn't think there was anything wrong with it. I looked over at his sticking out of his pants. His didn't look anything like mine. I shrugged my shoulders. "There's nothing wrong with it. That's the way it looks."

After that strange conversation I decided to use the boys' room only if the stall was available.

Two years later I tried out for the junior high school football team. I was a small kid, but my father had been a junior varsity quarterback when he went to my school, so I thought maybe I could play football and one day be a quarterback.

Of course every day ended with a couple of laps around the track, and I ran as hard as I could so I could shower before the other players got there. I would quickly towel myself off and put on my underwear even if I was still wet. That way they wouldn't see my strange, abnormal penis. The football coach said I was pretty fast and suggested I try out for the track team instead of football, which was kind of nice.

While I was dressing to go home, I noticed the other players as they walked in and out of the showers. Not one of the them had a penis like mine. One guy had a curved one, but no one made fun of him, because he was one of the best defensive players.

After a couple of weeks of running the two laps like crazy, I decided to take it a little easier. I was still very self-conscious about my penis, but nobody made fun of me or asked me why it looked that way, so it didn't bother me enough to quit football.

When I was fifteen, my family moved to Austin, Texas, and I attended David Crockett High School. Crockett was a big school. Close to twenty-five hundred students. Trying out for the football team was way out of the question, so I tried out for the gymnastics team instead.

After practice everybody hit the showers, not just the gymnastics team but most of Crockett's athletic teams: wrestling, track, soccer, basketball, and sometimes the football team.

So here I was at a new school that didn't have just Mexican American students—it had whites, African Americans, and Asians. The school had everything.

With this many students from so many backgrounds there was much to learn and see. And one of the things I wanted to see was if anybody had a penis like mine.

There were all kinds of penises. Some looked like mine and others looked like the ones back home. It didn't seem to matter what your skin color was, though I did notice more white guys with penises like mine than Mexican Americans or Afro-Americans. Hmmm, this really puzzled me.

After thinking about this for weeks, I concluded that you're born with the penis God gave you and that's that. But I was still a little self-conscious about my penis.

A few months later my best friend from Edcouch came up to see me. It was good to see him, and I told him how strange it was to be around the white and Afro-American guys. I was so used to being around just Mexican Americans all my life, and I was still trying to get used to my new surroundings.

He asked me if I had gone out with any of the white girls, and I told him that I didn't think they liked Mexican Americans. He nodded when I said that. "Yeah, those white girls like it circumcised," he said. He put out his hands and pointed with both index fingers, keeping the distance between his fingers about a foot apart, to tell me what white girls liked. I knew from the commonly known gesture what he was referring to, so I played along. "Yeah, like those white guys have. Not like us," I said laughing.

However, I didn't know what "circumcised" meant. I had never heard the word before, but I knew that whatever it meant, it applied only to white guys.

Eight years passed, and I had become quite comfortable with my penis. I was in love and dating a wonderful woman who seemed to like my penis just fine. She made me completely forget Lolita's and Fide Flores's comments.

One night as we lay in bed my girlfriend began to play doctor with my private parts. She would take the head of my penis and lift it and let it fall down. She did this a few times and giggled each time it fell back down. She told me she was trying to see if it fell more to the right or more to the left. (Her findings were that it fell more to the right.)

She asked all sorts of strange questions about my penis. "Doesn't your tally whacker feel weird hanging there?" (That's where I got the expression, "tally whacker." She was from Arkansas and she told me that was what they called it up there. But I think the name "dingy whopper" is just as funny, and I got that name from a wild girl in Dallas.) "Did you ever get caught in a zipper? Does it get cold in the winter and hot in the summer?" All I knew was that I had never got my tally whacker caught in a zipper.

She played with it for a couple of minutes longer, and then, in a pleased voice, said, "You know what? I'm glad you're circumcised."

The small, cocky grin on my face fell right off. I jumped out of the bed and shouted at her, "What did you say?"

She said nothing and gave me a confused frown.

"What did you say about my tally whacker?" I shouted again.

Again she looked confused. "What? I said I like it."

"No, no, that's not what you said!"

"David, I said I like it," she repeated.

"No, that's not what you said," I said, shaking my head. "You said I was circumcised."

She looked at me and threw her arms up as if to say, No shit. "You are! Why do you think it looks like that?"

Suddenly I became very aware of my funny-looking penis. "I'm not circumcised. I'm Mexican, and there's nothing wrong with it. It's just the way it is."

She shook her head. "I didn't say there was anything wrong with it, David. I told you I was glad that you were circumcised."

"I'm not circumcised!"

She was still for a moment and looked at me with a small smile. "You didn't know you were circumcised, did you?"

I didn't say anything; I just looked at the legs of the bed.

"David, there's nothing wrong with being circumcised. It just means that when you were a baby the doctor cut off your foreskin," she said. "Your parents probably told him to."

I couldn't move. I just kept my eyes on the legs of the bed. She put out her hand. "Come here." I walked over and sat next to her, and she put her arm around me.

"I thought only white guys were circumcised," I said.

She shook her head and laughed. "Sometimes you can be real dumb."

From that day on I picked up where I had left off when I was eight. I went back to being a pretty normal, healthy kid with too much energy.

El sapo

No one could throw a frog as high as I could. Not even Orlando Álvarez, who was taller and stronger, could throw a sapo higher. I knew how to hold a sapo right. Just like throwing a terremote, except a sapo doesn't fall apart in the air.

Finding sapos was easy in my neighborhood. I lived in Edcouch, Texas, a small town in the Rio Grande Valley just one hour from the Gulf of Mexico, and when it rained, it rained long and hard. After a good hard rain, the ditches in front of our frame houses would fill up. The dirt from the gravel roads would follow the rain into the ditches, making the water look like thick chocolate milk.

In these muddy waters, my brother and I would play football with our friends, splashing through the charcos with a slippery, wet football until our mother would yell at us. She would swing open the front screen door and scream.

"¡Huercos cochinos! Get out of that charco! ¡Parecen marranos!"

It was in these charcos where we would find sapos. They were easy to locate because they made that loud, low croaking sound. And once we found them, they couldn't get away because they were slow and we were many. We were usually in a gang of four or five, and we'd surround the sapo and catch it. It was really something if one of us caught a sapo in the middle of its hop. Once we had captured a sapo, it would wiggle and squirm, but it was of no use. It would stop after a minute and just sit there without an expression.

I would make sure that the sapo was the size of my palm so I could ensure a good throw. Also, it was important that its legs and arms fell between my fingers. If we caught a sapo that was too small, we'd put it in a box for other uses. After catching a sapo that was just right, I would stand next to the tall palm tree in my neighbor's yard. I'd look up at the leaves of the tall palm tree. The outline of the leaves looked like curved blades against the cloudy sky. Then, with all my strength, I would throw that sapo.

"Eeeeee-loooooo," my brother and friends would say with glee and awe. That sapo would fly high, as high as the palm tree. It would reach its zenith and then stop for a second. In that second, my brother, my friends, and I would stand there looking up at the weightless sapo, its arms and legs stretched out as if it were going to fly away like a bird. But no. It would come down as fast as it went up. "¡Palo!" It would hit the damp ground; no blood, no screaming sounds like cats make when you throw them, and no expression on its gray green face. It would just lie there—dead.

"Eeeeeee-loooooo! Ese sapo went high," they would say with amazement. We'd all laugh. "Let's go look for some more sapos!"

And so the day would be devoted to finding sapos and thinking of new ways to have fun with them. We'd play catch with sapos. We'd tie kite string around them and swing them like a sling, watching the poor sapos fly across our yard trailing a kite string. They would hit the ground, bounce, and lie motionless. We'd shoot them with BB guns. We'd sit there with our BB guns and watch the sapo and wait till it croaked. Its neck would get big with air and we'd take aim. One block from our house was Highway 107, and that highway was built for cars and sapos. We'd take them out to Highway 107 and place one in the middle of the double yellow lines. And if it managed to hop off the highway safely, we'd put it back in the middle of the double yellow lines.

One weekend my parents went to San Antonio to visit our aunt and uncle and left my brother and me with our older cousin, Berta. She was from Weslaco and was supposed to be real smart. Berta was nice and she could drive a car. Our parents left Friday afternoon, even though it was raining, and that night Berta let us stay up till midnight and watch TV. All night it rained, and through the sound of the rain we could hear the sapos croaking loud.

On Saturday mornings, our friends would get to our house around nine o'clock. When they did, we all had to go outside. We weren't allowed to play in the house because we always seemed to break something. Outside, the sky was still cloudy and dark. The ground was damp, and the charcos were full of muddy water and full of sapos. First, we played football in the charcos. Cousin Berta said it was bueno to play in the charcos, but we had to hose ourselves off outside before going in the house. It was fine with us, because then we could have a water fight. After playing football for a while, our attention turned to the sapos. We'd walk through the charcos with a box, looking for them. We caught a sapo for each person and went to the palm tree. What we didn't know was that Berta was watching us from the screen door. I was going to throw first since I could throw the highest, and inside I felt that maybe I could throw this sapo past the leaves of the palm tree. I took a couple of deep breaths and threw as hard as I could. I watched that sapo fly. Then we heard a scream.

"Eeeeeeee! ¿Qué están haciendo?" Berta came running out of the house. She let out a scream as the sapo flew straight up. The sapo reached its zenith just past the highest palm leaf. Berta's eyes were fixed on the wingless sapo. Like the others before, it came flying down as fast as it went up. ¡Palo! Its gray green body hit the damp ground.

"What's wrong with you? You just killed that poor sapo. Why did you do that?" Berta asked in an angry tone. My friends stood still, saying nothing. My brother looked at me. I looked at Cousin Berta.

"It's just a sapo!" I said.

Berta placed one hand on her hip and pointed at me with the other. With her finger pointed at me, she jabbed the air between us with each word.

"¡Ah sí! Cómo te gustaría if I threw you up in the air and watched you die?" Berta said. "Look at that sapo! You just killed it, por nada!"

"No más son sapos," I said. "Mira, the charcos are full of them." I pointed to the ditches filled with muddy water. My brother and my friends were as confused as I was. They stood there looking at Cousin Berta, each with a sapo in his hand, ready to throw. Cousin Berta's eyes quickly scanned them, and she saw the remaining sapos surrounded by fingers. Sapos with no expressions, trapped in the hands of "huercos cochinos."

"Put those sapos back in the charco!" she said, pointing at the charco.

"Pero, Prima, they took a long time to catch," my brother said.

"¿Sabes por qué? Because they don't want to be caught and tortured," she said. "Ahora, put those sapos back in the charco right now!"

"All of them?" I asked.

"¡Sí, todos!" she said.

"Even the ones in the box?" I asked.

"What box?"

Orlando pointed to the box by the palm tree. It was the box with the small sapos. Cousin Berta immediately walked over to the box, and when she saw the small sapos sitting in the box, she bit her lower lip and looked like a dog growling.

"Put all these sapos, all of them, back in the charco!" she said. Cousin Berta looked pretty mad, so we did what she said. Orlando was going to throw his sapo at the charco from where we were standing, but Cousin Berta didn't let him. We let all the sapos go back into the charco, and we turned the box of sapos over into the charco. Sapos hopped and swam to their freedom.

After all the sapos were free, Cousin Berta made our friends go home and told my brother and me to get in the house. My brother and I spent the remainder of the afternoon watching TV, and for supper Berta made tacos. The kitchen had the warm aroma of corn tortillas and carne. At the center of the table was a bowl filled with lettuce and tomatoes, and on each plate were three hot, greasy tacos. Cousin Berta didn't look mad anymore and she was being nice to us.

Outside it was dark, and the cool, damp night air flowed through the kitchen screen door. Every now and then we could hear cars and eighteen-wheelers passing on Highway 107. The cars that passed in front of our house drove slowly, their tires breaking the rocks of the gravel road. Invisible dogs were barking at something they saw or smelled. But what we could hear the most were sapos croaking. The long, low moaning sounds were continuous. As if there were a choir of sapos singing, "Row, row, row your boat." Cousin Berta leaned back in her chair and looked at us. We were happy, my brother and I. Cousin Berta wasn't mad anymore, and our stomachs were full of tacos.

"Esos sapos are sure making a lot of noise tonight, aren't they?" she said. My brother and I looked at each other as if to say, Where did that come from?

"They always make noise," my brother said.

"Sí, pero, they don't always make that much noise."

"Well, yeah, they're sapos. They're supposed to make noise. They don't do anything else," I said.

"No, sapos do more than just make noise."

"Bueno, they hop and swim and sometimes they pee on you," I said. My brother and I laughed, but my cousin Berta didn't laugh. She just looked at us with a small, scary grin.

"Do you know why I think those sapos are making so much noise? Because I think they're mad at both of you. And tonight, when you are sleeping, they're going to get inside this house and kill you!" she said in a very serious tone. My brother looked at me and I looked at him. We both started laughing.

"¡No, hombre, no! I'll give ese sapo un patazo!" I said. My brother followed my bold statement.

"¡No, que no!" We both laughed. Cousin Berta didn't laugh; she just looked at us with a small grin.

"Have you ever seen a sapo inside your house?" Berta asked. My brother and I were still laughing over the thought of a sapo trying to kill us. "You have, haven't you," she continued.

"Yeah, we've seen a sapo in the house," my brother answered. "But it didn't try to kill us!" My brother continued laughing. Cousin Berta looked a little mad, but she didn't say anything; she just waited till we stopped laughing. Gradually our laughing became giggling, and then just a hee and a ha here and there.

"Remember that dead baby they found in Weslaco? Remember?" she asked. We sat still trying to recall the exact events surrounding the famous dead baby. The Valley newspapers ran stories on the dead baby, and doctors tried to figure out how the baby died. But no one really knew.

"Do you know your tía Carmen's friend, Lucía?" Berta asked. We knew Lucía very well. Tía Carmen and Lucía were good friends, and everybody in Weslaco would see Lucía to get cured. See, Lucía was a curandera and everyone in Weslaco respected her.

"When the parents found their baby in the crib not breathing, they called Lucía first," Berta said. "¿Y sabes qué? Lucía said she found a sapo in the room where the baby was sleeping, and she also found a yellow stain on the baby's clothes."

We knew what the yellow stain meant. Sapos would sometimes pee on you if you held them wrong, and the pee would get your clothes dirty.

"Lucía said the sapo killed that baby, and there was nothing anybody could do to bring that dead baby back!" Berta said. My brother and I looked at each other. We weren't laughing and my brother looked scared and I was scared.

"Un sapo could get in this house tonight and kill both of you just like that sapo killed that poor baby," Berta said. "It comes in your house hopping very quietly and walks through the house smelling the air. Smelling the charco water in your hair. Then, when the sapo finds your room, it squeezes underneath the door. It watches you sleep. Then it jumps on your bed. It walks very slowly up toward your head. It gets on your chest and moves up to your neck."

Berta made body movements like the sapo would. She then put her hands out as if to grab us. "It grabs your throat with its little hands." Berta's hands grasped the air in front of us. "At the end of each finger, sapos have small suction cups and they won't let go of your neck. It will choke you to death!"

Berta looked at us. Her dark brown eyes looked black, and she just kept on looking at us. I looked over at Roger, who was right next to me, my shoulder touching his shoulder. Roger looked at me and suddenly his eyes became big.

"But I didn't kill any sapos today!" Roger burst out. "David killed lots of them today, but I didn't kill any."

"¿Qué? I only killed one today, and yesterday you killed lots of sapos. And you're always killing baby sapos," I said.

"Ya! It doesn't matter how many you killed," Berta said. "Ahora both of you go to bed. Ya es tarde."

We did as Cousin Berta said, and once we were in our room, Roger and I looked underneath our beds to see if any sapos were there. Nothing. We looked in the closet and in the trash can. Nothing. We felt a little better after having searched the room. But Roger was still a little nervous.

Outside the sapos were croaking, making low sounds that traveled through the window screens.

"They sound like they're right outside!" Roger said.

"Roger, they sound like that all the time."

I got up from my bed and closed the windows.

"Ya! Is that better now?" I asked, as if I only closed the window for his sake. Roger looked a little better, then his eyes saw the light. The light that squeezed underneath the door into our room.

"It can still get in here!" he said. "¡Mira!" Roger pointed to the thin light. He was right. Cousin Berta said that a sapo could get in a room by going under the door. Once again, I got up and turned on the bedroom light. I grabbed our big dictionary and the biggest encyclopedias. I stacked them against the foot of the door. They were heavy books, and I felt confident that no sapo could push those books aside. Roger and I slept well.

The next day my friends came over, and again we played football in the charcos. After a soaking game of football, Orlando picked up his BB gun and said, "Let's go shoot some sapos!" I looked at him and Roger looked at me.

"¡No, hombre, no! Let's shoot some gatos!" I said. And so we spent the rest of the day hunting cats.

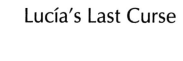

Lucía's Last Curse

Vicente couldn't run fast enough. She was gaining on him. This was the third night in a row that this woman had chased him. He was scared because he couldn't make himself wake up.

In his dream he would look back at her as he ran. He could see her face clearly. Her body moved with the cold wind that penetrated his naked body. With her arm extended and hand open, she touched his bare shoulder. The touch of her clammy skin would jerk his body so violently that he would awake.

Eddie came into Vicente's room.

"You all right, man?" he asked.

"Of course, I am not all right, man," Vicente said. "I feel like shit."

"Yeah? Well you're also making crazy chicken sounds," Eddie said. "Did you have another one of those bad dreams?"

Vicente slowly shook his head and let out a quiet sigh. His roommate and friend of fifteen years had never seen him look so sick. Eddie shook his head and shrugged his shoulders.

"You look like shit, man," he said. "What did the alcoholic doctor at the student health clinic say?"

Vicente coughed a bit and let out a weak laugh. "He gave me a shot of something and told me to practice safe sex," he said.

"Did you tell him that you always wash your hands before having sex with Manuela?" Eddie said, letting out a small laugh.

Vicente laughed and coughed. Eddie was trying to make him feel better, but he knew that Vicente was really sick.

"Listen, man, I better call your mom," Eddie said. "You really don't look good. I think you better go to the hospital. It's that or go to a veterinarian so she can put you to sleep."

"Shit, man, I can't afford going to the vet, much less to a hospital," Vicente said.

"Yeah, well get some rest, man. I'll call your mom and get your homework from the profs. Okay?"

Vicente nodded slowly and pulled the covers up above his shoulders.

Eddie called Vicente's mother down in Corpus Christi to tell her how sick Vicente was. She was a worrier, and Eddie did his best to make it sound as if Vicente wasn't that sick, but sick enough.

"Has he been to the doctor?" she asked.

"Yes, Mrs. Rodríguez, he has, but he is still sick, and it's been like this for almost a week," he said.

"Eddie, can you please bring him home tonight?" she asked. "And I'll take care of him, ¿bueno?"

"Sure, Mrs. Rodríguez, whatever I can do."

Mrs. Rodríguez hung up the phone and thought for a few moments. Her poor son was always getting sick, and everything seemed to happen to him. Mrs. Rodríguez thought that maybe what Vicente needed was a curandera, but she didn't know any good ones in Corpus Christi. She decided to call her sister in the Valley. Viola always knew what to do.

Viola listened to her sister, and when she heard the idea of asking a curandera for help, she knew exactly whom to ask. Viola knew a young woman, Anna, who attended Pan American University and helped her around the house. Anna's mother was the best curandera in the Valley. Viola told her sister that she would ask Anna if her mother would be willing to drive to Corpus to cure Vicente.

Later that afternoon, when Anna came to the house, Viola told her how sick Vicente was and asked if her mother would be nice enough to go up to Corpus and see if she could cure him.

Anna had worked for Viola for over a year and had met Vicente a few times. She was only two years older than Vicente, and she liked him and felt a strong sense of family when they were together. So she readily agreed to ask her mother.

Lucía was a woman whom many of the old people in the Valley feared. She had strong healing powers, and some said she had also practiced negro when she was younger. Lucía lived outside of Hargill, a small town twenty miles from Edinburg, way out on a rancho. Nobody lived around her because the farmers said the land around her house was not good for growing anything but bruja plants.

Lucía was used to being called names. Most of her life she had been a woman who practiced negro. She was known to have powerful curses at her command. She could make it so that a man could not get an erection so he could not cheat on his wife or girlfriend. It was even said that she had performed abortions on women from across the border.

But that was then, and now all the work she did was good. Every night she prayed to the Virgin Mary for the power to heal. In her soul, deep in her soul, she wanted to be forgiven for her evil past.

When Lucía heard of Vicente's illness, she saw it as one more good deed to counter the evil deeds of her past. Her daughter said it would involve a trip to Corpus Christi, but Lucía felt a little getaway would be nice. And besides, Viola was good to Anna and always paid her on time.

Mrs. Rodríguez was happy to hear that Viola had found a curandera so quickly, and she began to clean the house for her guests. She knew that Lucía was in her early sixties and expected that Viola and Lucía would probably spend the night.

Eddie could see that Vicente was having a difficult time keeping his head up. Vicente had not had a decent night's sleep since he had gotten sick, and the bad dreams made it only worse.

"Hang in there, man, we're almost home," Eddie said.

Vicente could say nothing. He just nodded his head slowly. By six o'clock they arrived at Vicente's house.

Mrs. Rodríguez came out and helped Eddie bring Vicente into the house. Vicente's body had given in to the illness, leaving him no strength to walk. He was glad to be home, a place where he knew he would be loved and cared for.

That night Mrs. Rodríguez made soup and fed her son, one spoonful at a time. She put a cool, wet towel on his head to keep his fever down and stayed with him until he fell asleep.

Anna and her mother arrived in Edcouch by eight o'clock in the morning. Viola had made some coffee and bought some barbacoa for breakfast. When the women arrived, they ate breakfast and talked about how much the Valley had grown in the last few years. Viola noticed that Lucía had brought a small, black suitcase and figured it had to be some overnight clothes.

Viola was a little nervous; she felt a strange energy coming from Lucía. She felt as if the priest were over for breakfast, but Lucía's energy was different. Viola felt as if her house had others present besides the three of them. Others looking and walking through her house.

By nine o'clock, Viola and Lucía were on their way to Corpus Christi. Both women said a small prayer before leaving. Lucía mumbled a few extra words in Spanish that Viola couldn't make out.

It was a cool November day in southern Texas with blue skies and feather clouds riding the high, cold wind streams. Lucía gathered her black shawl around her and looked up at the sky. "It's going to be a cold winter," she said softly to herself.

During the drive Lucía asked simple questions, asking where Viola was from and where her mother was from. Viola said that she was from San Benito, but her mother was from San Marcos, and that's where both her parents now lived. Lucía nodded.

"Ah, how long have they lived in San Marcos?" Lucía asked.

"Most of their lives. They only lived in San Benito a couple of years," Viola answered. Lucía nodded.

The rest of the drive was the same; every now and then another simple question, and Lucía would nod her head.

Mrs. Rodríguez was glad to see her sister and gave her a hug. Viola introduced Lucía to her sister, who extended her hand with a warm smile.

"Gracias a Dios que veniste, Señora Lucía," she said.

Lucía nodded. "I hope with God's help I can heal your son, Mrs. Rodríguez."

Mrs. Rodríguez smiled. "Please, Señora Lucía, you can call me Becky."

The women made their way into the house. Lucía carried her black suitcase, and as she entered the house made the sign of the cross and mumbled some words in Spanish.

Vicente could hear the women's voices through the wall. He could make out his aunt's voice but couldn't make out the third. His body quivered and shook, sending goosebumps across his hot body.

Lucía sat down on the sofa and looked around the living room. Mrs. Rodríguez asked if she wanted anything to drink or eat. Lucía asked for a glass of water. Mrs. Rodríguez walked into the kitchen to get a glass of water.

"Viola tells me you lived in San Benito for two years," Lucía said.

"Yes, yes, we lived in San Benito for a while. Then I got married and moved here to Corpus Christi, and Viola also got married and moved to Edcouch," Mrs. Rodríguez said.

"¿Y tu esposo es de San Benito?" Lucía asked.

"No, he is from Corpus Christi, but he lived with his grandmother in San Benito for a while," Mrs. Rodríguez said. "We got married here in Corpus and stayed here."

Lucía nodded and let her eyes casually search the room for photos of Mrs. Rodríguez's husband.

"Lucía, are you sure you don't want anything to eat before you try to heal Vicente?" Mrs. Rodríguez asked as she gave Lucía the glass of water.

"Gracias, but not right now," Lucía answered. "I feel strong today."

Mrs. Rodríguez smiled and watched her drink the glass of water. She thought that Lucía looked much older than sixty; more like in her early eighties. Lucía looked old and tired, but her eyes still had a sparkle to them.

"I think I'm ready to meet your son," Lucía said. "I'd like to see if I can heal your boy. With God's help, I hope I can." The women got up and Mrs. Rodríguez led the way to Vicente's room. Lucía carried her black suitcase and kept looking around as she walked through the house.

Vicente could hear light footsteps coming down the short hall. He tried to figure out who the third woman could be; though he felt he knew her, he wasn't quite sure.

Mrs. Rodríguez gently knocked on the door. "Vicente, are you awake?" she asked, opening the door. Vicente couldn't believe his mother was bringing in his aunt and the other woman without giving him a chance to brush his teeth or comb his hair. At least he was wearing the Johnny Carson pajamas he had gotten for Christmas a couple of years ago. He sat up and scooted to the head of the bed, trying to make himself somewhat more presentable.

Viola went up to him and gave him a hug and a kiss.

"I am so sorry you're sick, m'hijito, but after today you're going to feel much better," Viola said with a smile.

Vicente smiled back, not sure what his aunt was talking about.

"Vicente, I want you to meet Lucía," his mother said. "She's from the Valley and she's here to cure you." Vicente nodded slowly. "From the Valley?"

"Sí, m'hijito, she came with me," Viola answered. "Lucía is Anna's mother, and Anna asked her to come here to cure you. Lucía is the best curandera in the Valley."

Vicente said nothing for a moment. He was trying to figure out what his mother was up to. Lucía stepped forward, closer to him, so he could get a better look at her. She smiled at him, and again he felt as if he knew her.

"How do you feel, Vicente?" Lucía asked.

"Not too good," he said. "I am very weak and my chest and throat feel sore. I think it's from all the coughing."

"Yes, Lucía, he was coughing all night," Mrs. Rodríguez said.

Lucía walked up to him and put her hand on his forehead.

"You feel hot," Lucía said. "Does your head hurt, too?"

"Yeah, a little bit. Yeah," he replied.

Lucía stepped away and then turned to the women. "Becky, I need to talk to your son alone for a little while," she said. "I need to ask him some questions before I start."

The women agreed to her request, but before leaving the room, Mrs. Rodríguez turned to Vicente and told him to do as Lucía asked. Lucía closed the door behind the women and picked up her black suitcase. She pulled a chair from behind Vicente's desk and sat down, putting the small case by her side.

Lucía said nothing for a moment and simply looked at Vicente. Such a handsome boy, she thought.

"How old are you, Vicente?" she asked.

"I'm twenty-one."

"Ah, Anna is just two years older than you," she said.

"Yeah, Anna is real nice," he said.

"Bueno, you are not doing so good, eh?" she said. "Your tía says that you are always getting sick. Is that true?"

Vicente readjusted himself in the bed. "Not always, but when I was kid I got real sick a couple of times."

Lucía nodded. "Sick; like how were you sick?"

"Well, when I was a kid I got pneumonia twice and . . ."

"Twice?" Lucía raised her brow.

"Yeah, they say if you get it once it's easy to get again," Vicente said.

"Ah, bueno. Go on."

"So I got pneumonia twice, and I'm allergic to a lot of stuff, and I had my appendix taken out when I was about thirteen," Vicente said. "Then there was the time I almost had knee surgery, but I didn't."

"You have bad knees?" Lucía asked.

"No, I don't have bad knees. It's that I fell down and twisted my leg," he said. "It's okay now."

"How did you fall down?"

"I was being chased by a dog and it bit me and I fell," he said.

"The dog bit you on the same leg?" she asked.

Vicente sighed. "No, he bit my butt."

"Ah, that hurt, eh?"

Vicente nodded. Lucía sat for a moment and wondered how such a young man could have such bad health and bad luck.

"Did you ever break a bone, like your arm or something?" she asked.

"Yeah, I have had a couple of fingers broken, my right arm, and my left foot," he said. Lucía nodded her head as if to say, Go on.

Vicente wondered how much more medical history this woman would want. Vicente sighed again. He held out his right arm and with his left hand held the last two fingers on his right hand.

"I broke these two fingers playing baseball when I was in Little League," he said.

"Did you fall down like you did when the dog chased you?"

"No, no, I was, ah . . . I was up to bat and the pitcher pitched the ball and it hit my two fingers and broke them," he said.

Lucía made a face of disbelief. "And your arm?"

Vicente nodded. "Yes. I broke my arm jumping hurdles when I was in track in high school."

Lucía frowned a bit and shook her head. "You fell down?" she asked.

"Yeah, I fell down. I was running, and when I jumped I didn't jump high enough, and my legs got caught in the hurdle somehow, and me and the hurdle got all twisted up, and somehow my arm got caught in the hurdle and it broke," Vicente said, moving his hands around trying to explain how the accident occurred.

Again Lucía made a face and shook her head slowly. Why did this boy have such bad luck, she thought to herself. Vicente looked at her and began to wonder how he had managed to stay alive this long.

"Y tu foot?" she asked.

Vicente sighed again and slowly nodded his head. "Yeah, my foot. Well, when I was ten years old, my father died and . . ."

Lucía's body stiffened. "Your father died? I thought your father was still alive."

"No, my ex-stepfather is still alive, but my real father died."

Lucía looked at the floor and thought for a moment. "What was his name?"

"My real father or my stepfather?" Vicente asked.

"Your real father."

"Román Guzmán, and my stepfather is Luis Rodrí—"

Román Guzmán. The name sent Lucía back twenty-two years to the time of her dark, evil soul. Her body chilled as she felt her weak heart let out a sad cry. She closed her eyes and thought, How many more, God? How many more wrongs must she endure for her foolish past? Maybe it wasn't the same man? Maybe this boy's curse would not strike her. She opened her eyes and saw the confusion in the boy's face. She regained her composure.

"Perdóname, please tell me what you were saying."

"Are you all right? Do you want some water or something?" Vicente asked. "Want something to eat?"

"No, I'm okay. Just tell me what you were saying."

Vicente shrugged his shoulders and went on. "Well, when my father died, I wanted to be one of the pallbearers. My mother didn't want me to because she thought I couldn't lift the casket, but I did okay," he said. "But my uncle, who was right across from me—we were the ones leading—well, he was drunk, real drunk, and somehow he lost his balance and fell towards me. Anyway, everybody lost their balance and fell, and we dropped the casket. I tried to hang on, and the casket fell on my left foot and broke it."

Lucía put her hands on her face and slowly brought them down around her mouth. Vicente could see the woman's eyes watering. Her eyes closed, and a tear followed the lines down her cheek. She mumbled something in Spanish and thought of the hate that once filled her soul. So much hate she had had for him that she had cursed the innocent. What kind of woman would do that to the innocent? "Perdóname, Dios. Por favor, perdóname," she said into her warm hands.

She opened her eyes and wiped her tears. Vicente couldn't figure out what was wrong with this woman. Again she regained her composure.

"Vicente, do you have a picture of your real father?"

Vicente was getting confused and his head was throbbing. "Sí, Lucía. Do you want to see it?"

Lucía nodded. Vicente got up, walked to his closet, and took down a photo album. He sat down and thumbed through the pages. He took out a picture and handed it to Lucía. "That's my father."

Lucía looked at the old photograph. He looked just as she remembered him. That coyote smile and the thick, dark hair. What woman wouldn't hate him? She looked at his son. He would be proud of such a fine young man.

She could see that Anna had her father's eyes. How could she have cursed Anna's father? How could she have cursed his son, an innocent? She knew she was going to break down; she could feel her body trembling.

"Vicente, are you having bad dreams?" she asked.

"What?"

Lucía nodded her head slowly. "You're having bad dreams."

"Yes," he said.

"A woman is trying to get you," she said, nodding her head.

"Yes," he said.

Lucía picked up her black suitcase, opened it, and took out a small-change purse. She opened it and took out a photograph of herself when she was much younger. It was an old picture with bent corners and a couple of cracks running across it. She gave it to Vicente. "Do you know this woman?"

Vicente knew her. "This is her! This is her! This is the woman who is chasing me. How did you know?" he asked in disbelief. "Who are you?"

Lucía took a deep breath and got up. "I can cure you. I need to talk to your mother. You lie back down. I can cure you, but first I need to talk to your mother."

Vicente began to speak, but Lucía looked at him and in a firm voice told him to lie down. This time Vicente said nothing.

Lucía left the room and walked into the living room, where Mrs. Rodríguez and Viola were sitting. As she entered, they stood up. "Is he okay, Lucía? I pray that you can help him," Mrs. Rodríguez said.

Lucía sat down and the two women sat down as well. Lucía said nothing for a few seconds. She was trying to figure out how to explain it all.

"Your son has a very powerful curse on him. It is powerful because the curse on him was done in hate," Lucía said. "I can take the curse away, but both of you must promise me one thing. If you don't do as you promise, Anna might die."

Viola was stunned. "Anna? Why would Anna die?" she asked.

Lucía put her hands to her face and looked at the floor. She took a deep breath.

"Anna is not my daughter. She belonged to my sister, who died when Anna was born. Román Guzmán is Anna's father. When Román found out he got my sister pregnant, he stopped coming by and didn't even come to my sister's funeral. I was so mad and filled with hate for him that I put a powerful curse on him and his first son. That both of them have bad luck and bad health. My curse killed Román and now it's killing your son, Mrs. Rodríguez." Lucía began to cry.

Mrs. Rodríguez and Viola were without words.

"I will take the curse off your son, but you both must promise me that after I take the curse off, you will do what I ask," Lucía said. "I don't want my Anna to suffer for my sins."

Mrs. Rodríguez and Viola nodded their heads slowly with a look of disbelief.

"What I'm saying is true and God knows," Lucía said.

Lucía got up and went into Vicente's room. When she entered the room, he tried to get up.

"Be still, my son, I am going to cure you of an evil curse," she said. "You just lie there, and I will make your bad dreams go away."

Vicente said nothing and didn't move. He could feel the good in her. He wasn't afraid.

"Close your eyes and be still," she said.

Lucía first lit a white candle and then burned some incense. She began her prayer in Spanish. "Lo que yo deseo para ti, sobre mí ha de caer. Y la maldición se me ha de devolver." The room filled with the aroma of the burning plants. Vicente took a deep breath and could feel his body warm and his lungs fill with air. He felt lighter. Never had he felt so relaxed. She watched his chest rise and fall slowly. The smooth rhythm of his breathing told her that he was fast asleep.

In his dream Vicente could see her standing in an open field. He wasn't afraid anymore. She smiled at him and then she began to float in the air. Higher and higher she went, waving at him until her body disappeared in the clouds.

He looked to his side, and there was his father smiling at him. His father reached out and held Vicente's hand and they began walking.

Lucía saw the smile on Vicente's face and knew she was ready.

Mrs. Rodríguez and Viola were happy to see Lucía come out of the room. Lucía was smiling.

"Vicente will be fine, thanks to God, but now we must go to church and pray," Lucía said. "Please, we must go now!"

"What about Vicente?" Mrs. Rodríguez asked.

"He will be fine. He is dreaming and he is happy," Lucía said.

The women drove to Mrs. Rodríguez's church, St. Mary's. The afternoon sun illuminated the front of the church and its stained-glass windows, and the image of Christ rising spread across the pews. On entering the church, each of the women made the sign of the cross, and then Lucía told them what she wanted them to do.

"Now that I have taken the curse off your son, we must pray that it does not fall on Anna," Lucía said. "We must pray with all our strength that the curse comes back to me."

"What?" Mrs. Rodríguez said.

"Becky, Lucía is the one that put the curse on Vicente and Román," Viola said. "If she takes the curse off, it will come back to her or the person she loves most."

"The curse might go to Anna, so we must pray that it comes back to me," Lucía said.

Mrs. Rodríguez looked at Viola, then at Lucía. "But if the curse falls on you, can you cure yourself?"

"Lucía has to take in the curse. If this curse is too powerful, it could . . ." Viola tried to finish but was cut off by Lucía.

"Ya, we don't have too much time," Lucía said. "We must pray now that the curse comes back to me, por favor."

The women knelt in the first pew before the altar. Lucía looked at Mrs. Rodríguez and gave her a hug.

"Gracias for letting me cure your son," she said. "I hope you can forgive me for what I did to your husband."

Mrs. Rodríguez smiled and began to pray.

Lucía closed her eyes and began to pray also. She asked for forgiveness and prayed for the soul of Román Guzmán and of her sister. She prayed for an end to all her past curses. She prayed that this was the last curse.

Her body became light and she began to fly. She saw herself praying and saw the smile on her face as her body fell back into the pew. Mrs. Rodríguez and Viola began shaking her gently, but Lucía kept on flying.

El Cucúi

Roger and I were like other five- and six-year-old boys. We ran around yelling and screaming, chasing each other all day long like a dog chases his tail. We did this for no apparent reason, and if we weren't chasing each other, we were fighting or doing something equally loud.

Our parents both worked so it was hard for our mother to keep the house clean and keep one eye on us. So we had maids.

In the Rio Grande Valley having a maid was not as expensive as one might think. Every maid who worked for our family was a Mexican national, and most didn't speak a word of English, which didn't bother us because we were also Mexicans, except that we were born north of the border.

When we were growing up, we had maids that would quit working for us within months, sometimes weeks. We had five maids in all, and each one had different ways of trying to make us behave: mean stares, yelling, threats, bribes, begging, and the old standby, crying.

In the end they would give up, but not before telling our mother what they thought of Roger and me. They would say that we were traviesos, and one even thought we had the devil in us.

Cata, our last maid and the one who lived with us for more than six years, was very different from all the other maids. Her approach to controlling us involved reaching deep into our psyche and tapping our innate fear. The fear of El Cucúi.

Cata was a small, slim woman. She had long, black hair with lines of white running through it, but she mostly wore her hair in a bun so you couldn't tell how long it was, but it was long. She always wore a white Mexican dress and faded, white chanclas. Even when it was cold outside she wore the same thing, but with a blue shawl around her small shoulders.

Her skin was darker than my father's and her eyes were a deep brown. She was probably the oldest maid we ever had, but it was hard to tell how old she was because Mexican women don't show their age. My abuelita never looked her age.

The first night we were left alone with Cata, we decided to test her out. Cata was in the kitchen cleaning up, and Roger and I were running in and out of the kitchen just to annoy her. She said something about time to go to bed, but her voice was drowned out by our shouts and yells.

Then Cata dropped some spoons and forks on the floor. The sound of the metal spoons and forks startled us, and we stopped running and looked at her. She looked scared.

"¡Oye! Did you hear that?" Her brown eyes slowly moved to the backdoor and then to us. All we could hear was the chatter of the television.

"I don't hear anything," I said.

"Neither do I," Roger said.

"What you heard was the television," I said.

"Yeah," Roger said.

Cata walked over to the television, turned it off, and looked at us. "I heard something scratching at the door. I think it's out there."

"There's nothing out there. It's just the wind," I said with confidence in my voice. "Look, I'll even open the door and show you nothing is out there."

Cata's eyes got big and she began shaking her hands. "No, no, don't do that. Because that's what it wants you to do so it can grab you."

"What, what's going to grab me?" I asked.

Cata paused for a moment and looked at us. "El Cucúi is out there. Two of them, and they want to get both of you."

We both dropped our guard for a few seconds, then I, being the oldest, spoke first.

"There is no such thing as El Cucúi."

"Yeah, it's like Santa Claus. It's make-believe," Roger added.

Cata looked at us and nodded her head slowly.

"Ah sí, El Cucúi vive. El Cucúi knows you two are baaaad little boys and traviesos and that's why El Cucúi is outside waiting to get you," Cata said.

Roger looked a little worried, and I, too, was beginning to worry so I tried to reason out El Cucúi.

"El Cucúi is not real, my mother told me so," I said, though my mother had never said such a thing.

Cata raised her brow as if to say, ¡Ah sí! She placed her hands on her hips. "You believe in God, don't you?" Cata said, nodding her head.

Roger and I shrugged our shoulders and nodded. "Yeah," we both said.

"And God has angels, doesn't he?" We nodded yes again, following the motion of Cata's head.

"Bueno, now the devil has El Cucúi—not just one cucúi, but lots of them.

Every time a new soul enters the world, God gives that soul, boy or girl, an angel to protect them from all the evil in the world. If you are good, your angel helps you and protects you," Cata said with a small smile, but her smile faded as she proceeded. "But the devil is never too far.

"Bueno, the devil makes sure that for every new soul in the world there is a cucúi, and El Cucúi feeds off you. The meaner you are, the stronger El Cucúi gets, and then it comes to get you."

Roger and I were terrified. All I could hear was dogs barking down the street. Cata was smart. She knew she had us scared, but she wasn't finished yet.

"Do you know why those dogs are barking?" Cata asked.

Roger and I shook our heads.

"They know what cucúis smell like, and they're afraid because they know cucúis like to eat dogs. Sometimes, when dogs are missing, it's because a cucúi was hungry, and sometimes they eat cats, too," Cata continued. "Have you ever seen a cucúi ?" We hadn't and Cata knew it.

"They say El Cucúi is only as tall as you are, but they can be very strong. They have long claws on their hands and feet, and when they walk on floors or streets, their claws click and scratch. They can climb trees and the sides of houses very easily. They have small, sharp, pointed teeth, and saliva is always falling out of their mouths, just like with dogs or cows. They have long, pointed ears and can hear you whisper. They can hear you whisper bad, mean things. Some have red eyes and some have yellow eyes, and they look like cat eyes. They know what you smell like just like your dog knows. You can't hide from El Cucúi, but if you are good, he stays away."

Roger and I said nothing, and I didn't hear the dogs barking anymore. I looked into Cata's eyes and wasn't sure if they were brown or yellow. Roger and I were terrified.

I looked at the faded Palm Sunday cross hanging over our front door. And I looked at the living room wall where a painted picture of our Lord Jesus Christ hung. It was an image of Christ wearing a crown of thorns. Blood dripped down the side of his forehead, and his eyes looked up to Heaven. I looked at Roger, and he looked like he was about to cry.

"If we ask God to forgive us and are good, do you think El Cucúi will stay away?" I asked in a humble tone.

"I don't know. Only God knows. Now, it's time to go to bed, and don't forget to brush your teeth."

We brushed our teeth and went to bed and prayed that El Cucúi would eat Cata and not us.

She Wants to See the World

Gloria felt a little strange in the lesbian bar, but she didn't feel like being around men, so here she was in a bar where the women acted like men. She kept her eyes on her drink, watching the ice float in her vodka, knowing that if she looked up she would see someone from her company. A few of the women at work were lesbians, if not all, and everyone thought she was a lesbian, and the lesbians in her company were sure of it.

She could hear it now. "Guess what? I saw SFC Reyna at Aunt Jane's last night. I just knew she was." Gloria grinned at the thought as she jabbed the floating ice with her straw. With each stab the ice would sink but within a second float back up.

Country music flowed through the dimly lit bar as she sat at her table alone, watching women coming in wearing boots and some with cowboy hats on. They entered with a cocky stride. Gloria was very familiar with their walk—she could always tell which of the women were lesbians in her company. They usually were the best soldiers, even better than the men, but this was no surprise to her.

She got up and went to the bar to order a second drink. The bartender asked, "Same as before?" Sergeant Reyna nodded. "Yes." Back at her table she began thinking of her sisters, Dora and Isabel. They did what her father said they should do: graduate from high school, get married, and have children as soon as possible, but Gloria just couldn't see herself in that role, and besides there were no men in the Valley she would even consider marrying.

So in 1962, while still a senior at the Weslaco high school, she joined the army. Her parents weren't happy about the idea, and it took her two months to convince them that women who joined the army were not putas, jotas, or women looking for a husband.

"Why does a pretty girl like you want to join the army?" They asked. "Because I want to see the world," she told them over and over. Finally her parents signed the papers, and Gloria knew then that she had to prove she could do it.

Gloria was determined to be a good soldier. She pushed her five-foot-five, 110-pound body through camp and was sent to the Fort Sam Houston in San Antonio to be trained in the medical field. After two years of training she was sent to Vietnam. It was the first time in her life she felt real fear.

She looked at her hand holding her drink and let go of the glass to get a better look at the back of her hand. She put out both of her hands and studied the veins running along the top. They looked like her father's hands and she could see her age in them. Turning them slowly, as if she were opening a book, she looked at the deep lines in her opened palms.

When she was seventeen, Gloria and her best friend had gone to a palm reader, and the reader had told Gloria that she had a long life line, but a short love line. She tried to remember what line was what, the horizontal or the vertical, but it was so long ago.

Captain Anna Miller glanced over at Gloria's table. She wanted to make sure it was SFC Reyna before she went up to her table. Once Captain Miller was sure, she approached Gloria's table.

Gloria's eyes were following the lines in her palm when she heard the captain speak.

"Sergeant Reyna?"

The voice was familiar, and when Gloria looked up, she was not surprised to see Captain Miller. Gloria and Captain Miller would occasionally spot each other in the weight room of the army gym. She was a good captain and a smart woman, and she had gained Gloria's respect over the two or three years they had known each other. Gloria admired Miller's upbeat attitude in the gym and always mustered up one or two more reps when Miller spotted her.

"Captain Miller. How are you tonight?" Gloria asked with a nod.

"Can't complain, Sarge. And you?"

Gloria nodded as she placed her hands on the table and leaned back in her chair.

"No complaints here, Captain."

Captain Miller stood still for a moment as her eyes moved across the table and the empty chairs.

"Mind if I join you for a drink, Sarge, or are you waiting for someone?"

"No, no. Please have a seat, Captain," Gloria said with her hand held out.

"Thanks."

She sat down and leaned back in her chair, and the two women said nothing for a few seconds. Gloria was a little uncomfortable but knew her uneasiness wasn't showing. Her thirty years of military life had taught her control in awkward situations. Captain Miller was not sure how to start the conversation, and Sergeant Reyna was not one for small talk. Miller caught the attention of a waitress and asked Gloria if she wanted anything. Gloria said, "No thanks," and Miller ordered herself a drink.

"So, I've never seen you here. I'm a little surprised," Miller said.

Gloria nodded. "Well, the reason you've never seen me here is because this is my first time, and I'm even more surprised to be here."

"It's not a bad bar and the crowd is mature, not like some of those other bars, you know," Miller said.

"I wouldn't know, Captain. I usually stay home. I'm not much for loud crowds."

"Oh. Well, how did you hear about this bar? I mean, it's not a regular bar, you know."

Gloria was about to answer when she saw the waitress coming. She motioned to Miller. "Your drink, Captain." Miller paid the waitress and put a dollar tip on the tray.

The waitress smiled. "Thanks, Anna," she said, giving her wink.

Miller took a drink and set the glass down. "Anyway, how did you hear about this bar?"

"You told me about it."

Miller's body stiffened. "I told you?"

"That's right. One day in the gym you asked if I cared to have a drink with you after work. You said this was a bar where a woman could get some respect."

"I asked you if you wanted to have a drink with me?"

Gloria nodded.

"Wow, I must have taken a courage pill that day or something," Miller said. "And I told you this would be a good place, huh?"

Gloria nodded again and took a drink. The table was quiet for a few seconds while Miller thought of something else to say.

"So tell me, Sarge, what made you come here tonight?"

"I just didn't feel like sitting at home and don't like going to bars where men are. But don't get me wrong, Captain, I'm not a lesbian," Gloria said as she put her empty glass down on the table.

Miller looked into Gloria's cool, brown eyes, trying to see if there was truth to her words, but she couldn't read Spanish. The waitress broke the stare by asking if they cared for another drink.

"None for me, thanks. I'll be leaving soon," Gloria said.

Miller looked at Gloria and smiled. "Listen, it would be nice if you shared another drink with me, it's still early. What d'ya say? I'll buy this round."

Gloria exhaled and nodded. "Okay, Captain. Sure, one more."

"Great," Miller said.

They ordered their drinks and the waitress moved on. Miller smiled and put out her hand across the table.

"Listen, Sarge, it'd be nice if you called me Anna. I'd rather be on a first-name basis with you, and besides, we're not on the base."

Gloria returned the smile and put her hand out also. "I'm Gloria."

Anna shook her hand. "Pleased to meet you. My name is Anna."

The small gesture put Gloria at ease. She had always felt that Captain Miller would make a good friend, and this opportunity could be the start of a new friendship. She looked into Anna's light blue eyes and saw the honesty in the woman.

"So, Gloria, it'd be nice to know some things about you."

"What do you want to know?"

"Well, for starters, where are you from?"

"Well, I was born and raised in the Rio Grande Valley; it's about four hours from here. You know where Padre Island is?"

Anna nodded. "Yeah, that's close to Corpus Christi, right?"

"No, Corpus is a little further up the coast. Where are you from?"

"Born and raised in the great city of La Grange."

Gloria nodded. "That's right off I-10, isn't it?"

"Yeah, if you're going to Houston from San Antonio or Austin, you'll pass right by La Grange. Not a bad town, they got a lot of nice girls, but I don't think I'd ever want to live there again."

The waitress set the drinks down and Gloria tried to pay for her drink, but Anna wouldn't let her. "If you want, you can buy one later," she said.

Both women took a drink, and Gloria felt she should keep the conversation going.

"So you have no plans of one day moving back to La Grange?" Gloria asked.

"Are you kidding? When I was kid there, they practically ran me out of town. You know how boys get if pretty girls don't fall for their silly charms," Anna said. "Anyway, after I graduated from high school, I joined the army. My mother didn't like the idea, but she knew I could outrun half of the boys in school, so she figured I'd do all right."

"So how did you become an officer?"

"Oh, I stayed in for four years, got out, and used the money I had saved and the money Uncle Sam gave me, to go to college. Got my degree and went to OCS."

"That's great, Anna, I wish I had done that when I first got out of the army."

"Oh, you did the same thing?" Anna asked, looking surprised. "What made you get back in?"

"Well, I did the same thing you did; when I graduated from high school in 1962 I joined the army, got out in '69 and went back in '72, and I'm still here. I should have gone to college like you did, but I just wasn't thinking," Gloria said.

Anna nodded. "What made you get out and then get back in again?"

Gloria's eyes studied the table as her mind visited her memories. He was a handsome man, smart, too, but love during war is still a struggle, even when there's peace. She often wondered what she could have done, where she went wrong. Maybe if they had had a son or daughter things would have been different.

"Gloria," Anna said in a soft voice, bringing the music and smell of the bar back to Gloria.

"Sorry, I was thinking about your question. Ah . . . I got out because I was in love with this soldier I met over in Vietnam. He was a great guy and ah . . . I, I was pretty crazy about him. Love does that to you, makes you kind of crazy," Gloria said. "We came home and got married, which made my parents happy, but we both had trouble adjusting to civilian life and let out our frustrations on each other and . . . well . . . he . . . committed suicide, which was kind of funny being that he survived some crazy battles back in Vietnam. Anyway . . . that was a long time ago."

Anna said nothing for a moment; she felt as if she had ruined the evening for Gloria by evoking such memories.

"Gloria, I'm sorry about your husband and all, I didn't mean . . . "

"No, hey, that was a long time ago. You were probably just learning how to ride a bike back then," Gloria said with a smile.

"Huh, I wish. Heck, let's see, back in '69 I was fourteen years old and had the biggest breasts in my class to boot," Anna said with a smile.

"You were fourteen in 1969? I don't believe you, let's see some ID," Gloria said.

"Okay, let's see yours, too, because you don't look like you're in your forties."

"I'm not in my forties. I'm fifty," Gloria said with a slight shake of her head.

"Sure, let's see the ID."

The women traded IDs, and each began reading. Gloria read the information on Anna: Anna Louise Miller, born March 25, 1955; blue eyes; blond hair; height 5'6". Anna read Gloria's ID: Gloria Olivia Reyna, born December 21, 1945; brown eyes; brown hair; height 5'5".

"Well, Anna, I thought you were in your early thirties," Gloria said. "It must be all that time you spend in the gym that keeps you in such great shape."

"Keeps me in shape? You're the one that lifts more and does more reps, you're the one in great shape, and to top it off every man in the company thinks you're a knockout. Me, they just think I'm a dyke."

"I didn't think you were a lesbian when I first met you."

"You didn't?"

"No. No offense or anything, but you're attractive and look feminine to me, and I just thought you were kind of tomboyish but not a lesbian," Gloria said. "I mean, I've always been tomboyish myself and I just thought you were like me."

"Well, I am a lesbian and, no offense, but I thought or was kinda hoping that you might be like me," Anna replied. "I'm not trying to pick you up or anything like that, it's just that, well, like all the men in the company think you're a knockout, I also think you're a knockout."

Gloria said nothing, and Anna felt a little nervous and kept her eyes on her drink.

"Listen, I better leave before I make a fool of myself or say something stupid," Anna said. "I don't want you to get the wrong idea and then . . ."

"Anna, Anna, it's okay. I'm flattered that you think I'm a knockout," Gloria said. "But I like men, at least most of the time."

Anna nodded and smiled. "Yeah, they're okay every now and then," she said.

Both women were quiet again. Gloria was enjoying the talk. It had been a long time since she had sat and talked over a drink. Anna excused herself and went to the ladies' room, and Gloria watched her walk away. She had never seen Anna in bluejeans and boots. The Wrangler jeans were snug on her toned body, and her walk was a sexy cowgirl's walk, sure and confident. Her shoulder-length, blond hair was gathered back and held by a silver barrette, and her light blue Western shirt draped and folded around her body gently as she moved across the bar.

Gloria went back to her drink and smiled to herself. It was nice to hear that the men in her company thought she was a knockout. She looked up and could see herself in the mirror on the wall. Her hair was in a bun, and she thought that she looked a little uptight with her hair up. At least she didn't have a bouffant hairdo as some of the other women in her unit. She felt the need to let her hair down and pulled the pins out and let it flow down to the middle of her shoulders. Her scalp felt better and she felt better.

Anna walked up to the table and looked surprised. "Gloria? Wow, you look great. I've never seen you with your hair down. It looks great."

Gloria smiled. "Thanks, I just felt like letting it down."

"Well, in that case I'll let my hair down, too," Anna replied and removed her barrette. Her blond hair fell lightly around the sides of her face.

"I like having long hair, don't you?" Anna asked.

Gloria nodded in approval. "So do I. When I first joined, almost all the girls cut their hair, but not me," Gloria said with a smile. "It was a pain in the ass, but I just prefer my hair long."

"So do I. I think it's sexy to have long hair," Anna said. "Hey, Gloria, now don't take this wrong or anything, but would you like to dance a song or two?"

Gloria was surprised and could feel herself blushing as she smiled. She hoped it was dim enough so Anna couldn't see the color in her face.

"You want to dance with me?"

"Just once. It'll be fun."

"Well . . . I'm not much of dancer . . ."

"Don't worry about it. You're talking to someone from La Grange, Texas, where everyone can two-step blindfolded," Anna said with enthusiasm. "All you gotta do is follow my lead. What d'ya say?"

Gloria looked at the dance floor and saw women two-stepping together. Shuffling and spinning in each other's arms to the country music. It reminded her of when she was little and danced with her female cousins and friends at weddings. She looked back at Anna and studied her blue eyes, trying to see if it was a come-on or not. Again she looked at the women dancing across the floor and then back at Anna.

"Okay, Anna, but I'm warning you now, I haven't danced in years so I hope you're wearing steel-toed boots."

Anna laughed, and both women made their way to the dance floor. Anna held Gloria far enough away so that Gloria could follow the steps. Anna felt good dancing with her because Gloria was not just a woman but a lady, and ladies were hard to find.

"You're doing great, Gloria. Now let's try a few turns," Anna said.

Gloria followed Anna's lead and held firmly on to her shoulder. Anna held Gloria by her belt loop and gently clasped her hand. Gloria felt so good that she forgot she was dancing with a woman and that she was in a lesbian bar. All she knew was that Anna was leading.

Heart-Shaped Cookies

I was raised in a small south Texas town, a one-Catholic-church town, Edcouch, Texas. As you entered Edcouch on Highway 107, the sign read Entering Edcouch, Population 2,683. One mile later it read Leaving Edcouch, Population 2,683. But I don't think Edcouch really had that many people unless the sign took into account various farm animals and wandering pets.

I was no different from anyone else in Edcouch; I was Mexican American, spoke Spanish, and was Catholic. The Catholic church in Edcouch was St. Theresa, and it was in this church that I served as an altar boy.

The priest, Father Ortiz, loved me. I was his favorite altar boy, even though he once caught me and José Sosa eating a bag of unblessed Eucharist wafers. (Holy cookies, Joe and I liked to call them.)

I liked being an altar boy for two reasons. One, we were allowed to get out of school whenever Father Ortiz had to perform services at a funeral, which always meant a free lunch at the Dairy Queen. Two, every Sunday I got the chance to see just about everyone in Edcouch. Everyone except the "heathens," whom I saw at the five o'clock mass. The ten o'clock mass, though, had the most people, including a couple of the high school cheerleaders, who had to stick out their soft pink tongues to receive the holy cookie. There I would stand, next to Father Ortiz, with a small, round brass tray. When the girls would come up to accept the sacrament, they would close their eyes and stick out their pink tongues. What a sight that was!

St. Theresa had some interesting parishioners. There was the mayor, the fat mailman, who didn't deliver letters (we only had post office boxes in Edcouch), the policeman and his alcoholic brother, a few volunteer firemen, Mr. and Mrs. Carson (who were really Methodists), and Mr. Garza, the owner of the panadería. I liked most of the people who went to church, except Mr. Garza. Not even Luis Luna, the school bully, who lived in the worst part of Edcouch, el rincón del diablo (the devil's corner), was as mean as Mr. Garza.

During the collection part of the mass each altar boy would take one side of the pews. We only had two rows of pews, so we could cover the whole church. I always walked down the middle of the church and took the right side and always, always had to put the collection basket before Mr. Garza, who never gave a cent. The poorest woman in town, Miss Alvarado, who always wore a worn-out red shawl and an old pair of leather sandals and who only had three front teeth, always gave something. Even Luis Luna gave something, though it was probably stolen lunch money, but hey! he gave.

Anyway, Mr. Garza never gave. When I would put the collection basket in front of him, I would sometimes shake it a bit, but he wouldn't even flinch. This would go on and on, Sunday after Sunday. I would tell all my friends what a "pinche vato" Mr. Garza was.

My mother, as well as everyone else in town, loved Mr. Garza's panadería, and she would send me down to Mr. Garza's every other day to buy molletes, empanadas, and marranitos. I had to admit that Mr. Garza had great pan dulce: heart-shaped cookies covered with sugar and cookies shaped like pigs were my favorites.

As I pulled open the screen door to the bakery, a little bell above the door would jingle. You had to make sure the door closed behind you because Mr. Garza did not like flies in his bakery, and I don't think he liked me in his bakery either. Mr. Garza knew who I was, he knew my parents, and he always talked to my grandparents, but he never had anything to say to me.

There he would stand behind the glass counter with his fat, hairy arms resting on the counter. On his fat wrist he wore a gold watch, and gold rings circled his short, fat fingers. His hair was always slicked back and was as black as the thin, wormy-looking mustache underneath his pug nose.

He would look down at me and ask in a low voice, "¿Qué quieres esta mañana?" I would look in the glass cabinet filled with brightly colored molletes: pink, yellow, brown, red, and white. There were nice, big, brown marranitos, heart-shaped cookies covered with sugar, and pan dulce of all colors and shapes. I could feel my eyes dilating and my mouth watering. I would tell him what I wanted, pay him, and leave without saying any more than I had to. But I would make sure I was halfway home before I began eating the cookies because I did not want Mr. Garza to see me.

What probably made me the angriest was watching him drive by in his yellow Chevrolet Impala with his windows rolled up on the hottest days. Mr. Garza had a car with an eight-track tape player, a defroster, a heater, and an air conditioner, and they all worked.

One cold day after mass Father Ortiz invited the altar boys to his house right next to the church for hot Mexican chocolate and pan dulce. It was an invitation we couldn't refuse, and besides, you can't say no to a priest.

We were having a great time until I asked—knowing the answer—where he bought the cookies.

"What? I can't believe you bought the cookies from Mr. Garza's panadería," I immediately said. Father looked a little puzzled.

"Why, David, you don't like Mr. Garza's cookies?" he asked in his priestlike voice.

"No, I like the cookies. It's Mr. Garza I don't like, and you shouldn't like him either."

"Why don't you like Mr. Garza, David? Has he done something to hurt you?"

"No, it's just that he never gives money to the church. Whenever I put the basket in front of him, he just sits there."

Father looked a little upset and I knew why. I knew better: God doesn't care if you give money to the church or not, even if you are as rich as Mr. Garza. But instead of giving me the standard lecture, Father Ortiz asked me to follow him to his office. I figured he was going to give me the lecture in his office instead of in front of the other altar boys.

Once we were inside his office, Father Ortiz brought out a big, black book, one I had never seen before. It was full of names and I recognized all of them. They were parishioners of St. Theresa. Some of the names were in blue ink and others in red ink. Father pointed to Mr. Garza's name, which was in blue ink, and on the same line, a couple of inches across, was written the amount of $20,800.

"David, that's how much Mr. Garza has given to St. Theresa over the past eight years," Father said. "Do you know why he has given so much to the church?"

All I could do was shake my head—no.

"Nine years ago Mr. Garza's wife, Elena, became very ill and was dying. Mr. Garza and I prayed together all night for Elena. Mr. Garza made a promesa. Mr. Garza promised he would give the church fifty dollars a week for the rest of his life if God would let Elena live another year. Elena died four months after Mr. Garza made the promise."

I couldn't say anything. I felt terrible and asked Father to forgive me, but he said Mr. Garza was the one from whom I should ask forgiveness. After I found out about Mr. Garza's donations, I stopped shaking the collection basket in front of him, and I wouldn't say mean things about him to anyone. But I still could not say I was sorry for the things I thought. Weeks passed and months went by and then years, but I could not bring myself to apologize. Oh, I tried a couple of times, but I just couldn't.

Mr. Garza died three years ago, and marranitos and heart-shaped sugar cookies have never tasted the same.

Tina La Tinaca

Tina stood patiently in line. The wait gave her time to decide what she wanted from the menu board. Tina loved hot dogs with plenty of chile con carne and cheese.

The football stadium was filling up for the game between the Edcouch-Elsa Fighting Yellow Jackets and the Mercedes Tigers. The stadium lights gave the football field a bright, fresh, green color, almost glossy, and the white lines and numbers appeared to have depth. In Edcouch-Elsa, everyone went to the football games and cheered after every play.

Tina was excited about the game and she was proud of her new shirt, a gray, short-sleeved cotton T-shirt with the words "Edcouch-Elsa Fighting Yellow Jackets" printed on it in black and gold letters. The letters were stretched and distorted across her breasts and stomach because the shirt was too snug, but large was the largest size they had.

Tina ordered three hot dogs, a large popcorn, two large sodas, and a pickle for her son, Héctor. She walked slowly towards the bleachers, making sure not to drop her tray of snacks.

In one section of the stands a group of boys sat together ridiculing every person walking by. The girls were judged and then given a score between one and ten, one being "muy fea" and ten being "muy bonita." When they saw Tina walking by in her new T-shirt, one of the boys was quick with a comment.

"Ésa parece como el tinaco de Edcouch," he said. The boys laughed. From that first laugh, people in town referred to Tina as "Tina la Tinaca." Tina didn't know she looked like a water tower in her new, gray T-shirt. She just kept walking, looking for Héctor. Héctor kept an eye out for his mother, and as soon as he saw her, he waved his arms to get her attention. Once seated, they enjoyed the game.

Tina loved Héctor. She was grateful to God for the gift he had sent her. Héctor came to her through her brother, Rubén. Rubén was a borracho. His wife of three years had left him and Héctor, and he left Héctor with Tina. Rubén never came back, and so Héctor became Tina's son. Héctor didn't remember his father or mother very well, but he knew Tina and soon considered her his mother.

Tina was a happy person. She enjoyed her job at the health clinic, filing papers all day and answering the phone. She kept her files as neat as she kept her house. It was a nice, blue frame house with a clean yard and a colorful bed of flowers. She manicured her flowers weekly, and the man next door, Paco, mowed her lawn every couple of weeks for five dollars.

The inside of her house was as clean as her yard. On top of the television she had photographs of Héctor taken through the years and photos of them together taken at the Argüelles department store in Elsa. Her kitchen, too, was clean. Every morning she made breakfast for Héctor and herself. The kitchen would fill with the warm aroma of papas con huevos or chorizo con huevos, but no matter what they ate, there were always hot tortillas de harina. They would eat their breakfast, and somehow Tina always managed to clean the kitchen before going to work.

Héctor's room was no different from the rest of the house. When Héctor left for school in the morning, his room would be in a mess, but by the time he came home he would find his room clean. His room would not only be clean but in order. His shirts were all on hangers and his shoes paired up in a straight row.

Tina had decided that in the summer she would take Héctor to Houston. Héctor liked watching the Houston Astros baseball team on television, and she had always wanted to visit the Astroworld amusement park. Something for each of us, she thought.

Héctor was excited about visiting Astroworld and watching the Astros play in the Astrodome. He thought that maybe he should take his glove in case one of the players hit a foul ball or even a home run in his direction. He imagined catching that wild ball and everybody in the Valley seeing him catch it on KRIO-TV, channel 8, "home of the Houston Astros."

When he told his friends he was going to Astroworld and was going to watch the Astros play, most were impressed, but Lupe was a little jealous.

"How are you going to Houston?" Lupe asked. Héctor told him his mother was taking him.

"She's not your mother," Lupe said. "Tina is your tía!"

Héctor knew this was true, but Tina was still his mother.

"She's my mother!" Héctor repeated furiously.

"Tina is your tía! Your father was a drunk and left you with Tina. And your real mother left you, too!" Lupe said.

Héctor followed his emotions and charged Lupe. Both fell to the ground swinging and kicking. Héctor's glasses flew off his face. Héctor grabbed Lupe's shirt and tore it. Lupe managed to hit Héctor in the face, but didn't leave any marks. Both were pulled apart by their friends, but Héctor was still angry.

"¿Por qué te enojas? ¡Es la verdad! ¡Tina la Tinaca es tu tía!" Lupe said.

The boys began to laugh. It was the first time Héctor had heard the secret nickname everyone in town knew. Héctor felt like crying. He grabbed his broken glasses off the ground and began walking home. One of the boys called out to him to come back, but another quickly said to let him go.

Héctor told his mother he broke his glasses playing football. Tina believed him. Héctor now began spending most of his time at home, but it didn't bother him. He and Tina would go to church together, and every now and then they'd drive to McAllen to see a movie.

Within a few months Tina managed to save the money needed for the trip to Houston. She bought a Texas road map, and together they plotted their route. She laid out the map on the kitchen table but was confused by all the curved lines. She had never taken a trip by herself and knew she had to be confident in front of Héctor. With her stubby right index finger she pointed to the small dot on the map that represented Edcouch. "De aquí we want to go here." Her stubby left index finger landed on the big word, Houston.

While studying the map, Héctor began to worry that maybe they couldn't make the trip, but after seeing that it took only two major roads, Highway 77 and Interstate 59, to get there, he began to feel better. They would take Highway 77 through Raymondville, the Sarita checkpoint, Kingsville, and Robstown. In Victoria they would hop onto Interstate 59, which was a straight drive to Houston. They decided to take a small ice chest filled with sodas, cookies, tacos, and pan dulce.

On Friday morning Tina and Héctor left Edcouch. It was a comfortable drive because Tina's Chevrolet Impala had an air conditioner that cooled well. As they drove they ate the snacks they brought. Tina spun the dial on the radio looking for a station she and Héctor both liked.

By late afternoon Tina and Héctor arrived in Houston. Neither could believe the number of cars and how big the roads were. Some roads were four lanes and others were six lanes wide. Héctor even saw jets and helicopters flying in the sky, something he had never seen in Edcouch.

It was some time before they found a motel. The clerk at the counter said that Astroworld and the Astrodome could be seen from the second floor, so Tina asked for a room up there. The clerk was right. They could see the Astrodome's silver roof and the colorful neon lights of Astroworld. They both took a shower and later watched TV, flipping through the many channels, before going to sleep. In the darkness of the strange motel walls, Tina spoke to Héctor. "M'hijo, are you having a good time?" "Sí, 'ama, this is the best time I have ever had in my whole life!"

On Saturday morning Astroworld opened at nine o'clock, and they arrived with tickets in hand. They rode all the rides, and to Tina's surprise she could fit in every seat. She even saw several people who were bigger than she. Clearly, Tina was not as fat as she thought.

Tina saw a photo booth that had a cut-out, life-size picture of one of the roller coaster rides. Seated behind the picture, Tina and Héctor raised their arms as if on a roller coaster. They began to laugh. The photograph was ready in minutes, and they bought a blue frame with the words "Astroworld" in red at the top. Both were pleased with the photograph.

That night they watched fireworks blaze in the sky. They were the same type as those Héctor had seen on television at the beginning of each Walt Disney movie. The park closed at eleven o'clock, and they stayed until the last blaze.

The next day they got up early because they were excited about seeing the Astrodome. The baseball game started at one o'clock, but they were there by noon.

They walked around looking for their section. Héctor had seen the Astrodome on television dozens of times and was thrilled about watching a real, professional baseball game.

Tina found the concession stand and was pleased to see hot dogs on the menu board. The sodas came in plastic cups that had "Astrodome" and "Houston Astros" printed on them. This made Héctor very happy.

After the game they walked around in the parking lot of the Astrodome, searching for their car. Héctor saw their car first and began to run, weaving in and out between parked cars. Then he ran around a parked van and into the path of a slow-moving white truck. Héctor's eyes focused on the brightness of the Sunday setting sun, reflected off the chrome grill of the truck. Tina heard the short screech of the tires and the hollow metal sound the truck made when Héctor's body hit the hood.

Tina was in shock, and all she could say was, "M'hijo, m'hijo." She tried to get Héctor to talk. "M'hijo, m'hijo," she cried out, but not a sound came from Héctor's limp body. Within minutes an ambulance drove up. Two men jumped out. One man attended to Héctor, the other tried to talk to Tina. "Ma'am, is this your son?" he asked. "Ma'am, is this your son?" Tina could hear nothing; everything became twisted. She looked around and saw people surrounding her and the lights from the ambulance flashing blue and red. The ambulance drivers got another stretcher and laid Tina down on it.

Minutes later Tina was in a police car following the ambulance. The police officer was Mexican American but didn't speak Spanish. He asked Tina questions as they drove. "Where are you from?" "Where?" "Do you have any family here in Houston?" "Where is your car?" Tina could hear the questions, but her answers were slow. "I'm from Edcouch." "It's in the Valley." "No." "I left the car in the parking lot." The police officer assured her everything was going to be okay, but Tina didn't feel well. She was scared and confused.

At the hospital Tina was met by a social worker. She was a white woman, who spoke Spanish. "Yo hablo español," she said. She asked the same questions as the police officer, then asked if Tina had any family in the Valley, and what her religion was. Tina told her she had a brother, Rubén, but hadn't seen him in six years, and she belonged to the St. Theresa Catholic Church in Edcouch. The social worker had a police officer look up the town judge of Edcouch, thinking maybe the town judge could help.

Judge Gómez was a good man, and when he received the call from the social worker, he was quick to offer whatever help Tina needed. She told Judge Gómez that Héctor was not going to make it, because he had suffered too much brain damage. She also told the judge that he would receive a call as soon as Héctor died, and that Tina was in no condition to drive. "No problem," said the judge. "I'll have a couple of my police officers go up there and drive Tina back down."

Judge Gómez was worried for Tina. "Pobrecita," he said to himself. He knew how she felt about Héctor. The judge was the one who had signed the papers allowing Tina to become Héctor's legal guardian. He remembered how happy she had been when he signed the legal documents. "Gracias, muchas gracias, Judge Gómez. Que Dios lo bendiga," she had said.

Tina sat in the waiting room alone. She kept getting up and pacing the small room, rubbing her hands as she prayed in Spanish. The social worker entered the room with a priest and the doctor. The priest was Mexican American, and his skin was dark like Tina's. The doctor was a white man; he was lean, tall, and wore glasses.

"Tina, this is Father Víctor Sánchez and this is Doctor Crenshaw; they want to talk to you about Héctor," she said. Tina placed her hands in Father Víctor's hands and began to cry. She asked the priest to pray for Héctor, to pray that he'd be fine. The doctor was uncomfortable. He didn't understand Spanish, and he did not like being the messenger of death.

They all sat down on the waiting room sofas, and the doctor described to Tina how severe Héctor's head injuries were. He told her that Héctor would die in the next twenty-four hours, and that he had done the best he could, but it was all in God's hands.

Tina felt weak; the priest put his arms around her and said it was time to read the last rites to Héctor to prepare his soul for God's kingdom. He gave her a rosary to hold, and together they walked down the hall of the intensive care wing, passing rooms that held other patients living through machines. Héctor's bed was surrounded by others like him, people dying, connected to beeping and hissing machines.

The priest began his prayers, while Tina held Héctor's cold, little hand. Tina couldn't believe it was Héctor. His head was swollen and his face was blue, his dark brown eyes shut tight by the swelling. He didn't look like Héctor; she almost didn't accept it was Héctor, until she looked at his hands. It was *his* hand she held, it was *his* body, and it was Héctor who was dying. How she hoped this was all some terrible dream, but she could feel the cold air of the wing of the dying.

Judge Gómez called his two police officers, Julio and Joel Barco. They were brothers who had learned how to be policemen by watching television and movies. Judge Gómez wondered if they would ever get an offer to work in some other town. When the judge told them about Tina, one of them interrupted him. "You mean Tina la Tinaca?"

"No!" the judge snapped angrily. "I mean Tina." The Barcos stuffed their hands in their pockets and said nothing.

"Now listen," the judge said. "Héctor, Tina's son, has been involved in a car accident, and the doctors say he is not going to make it. I want both of you to drive up to Houston and bring Tina back, and if possible, the boy's body. The social worker up there says Tina is in no condition to drive. Understand?"

Both men nodded.

"Now, right now it's eight o'clock, and I want you two to take the city ambulance to bring back Héctor's body. You may want to put some bags of ice in the ambulance on the way back so the boy's body will stay cold." The judge thought for a moment. "Also, one of you will have to drive Tina back down in her car."

"Julio will drive her back down," Joel said.

"¿Qué? You're going to," Julio was quick to reply.

"No, hombre. Last time . . ." Joel was about to answer, but was cut off by the judge.

"I don't care who drives what. Just get it done! And when you get to Houston call me." Thinking to himself, the judge truly wished he could get some other officers.

Julio and Joel bought some snacks and cold beer for the trip. They drove the same route Tina and Héctor had driven two days earlier. On the way up they flipped a coin to see who would drive the ambulance and who would drive with Tina. Joel lost.

At four in the morning Judge Gómez received the call that Héctor had died. The judge talked to Tina and told her everything was going to be fine. "Tina, I'm sorry to hear about Héctor, but listen, the Barcos are on their way up there to bring you and Héctor back home. So don't worry about the trip, ¿bueno?" The judge also spoke to the social worker and explained that the Barcos were on their way, and that they had been instructed to bring Tina and Héctor back to Edcouch.

When they arrived in Houston, Julio and Joel drove around for an hour looking for the hospital. After a few wrong exits and many Wrong Way and No U-Turn signs they managed to find it. The social worker greeted them in the emergency room. "Bueno, buenos días," she said.

"Morning, I'm Joel Barco and this is my partner Julio Barco; we're here to pick up Miss Tina Guzmán and her son." Joel extended his hand. She shook his hand, then she shook Julio's hand.

"Yes, I'm Banford Wilson. I spoke to Judge Gómez just a couple of hours ago. He wants you to call him. Are you two brothers or something?"

"Yes, we're brothers," Julio said. "Where is Miss Guzmán, Miss Wilson?"

"She's in the waiting room; she hasn't slept all night, poor woman."

Tina sat on a chair in the waiting room unaware of the people around her. When she saw the Barcos walk in, people she knew, people like her, she began to cry.

"Julio, Joel, gracias a Dios que llegaron," she said in a breaking voice, her eyes watering. "Se murió mi hijo." Julio extended his arms to hug her and console her, but it was difficult for him to express his emotions. Her body shook in his arms, and he looked over at Joel, who shrugged his shoulders, not knowing what he should do. Tina didn't notice. She was relieved to have someone she knew there, in such a strange place, where pain had become part of the walls and death greeted one at the door.

"Tina, don't worry. We're going take you and Héctor back home. Bueno," Julio said. "Ya sabe el judge y el padre." Julio was trying to ease her pain, but he knew that he was not the best at this sort of thing.

"Sí, Tina, everything will be fine. Joel will drive you home and Héctor will ride with me," Julio said. "We brought the city ambulance so we could take the body, I mean, Héctor, back home." Tina nodded her head.

Arrangements were made with the hospital to allow the Barcos to take the body from the morgue, and Tina signed the necessary papers. Before getting the body, the

85

Barcos drove Tina to the Astrodome to pick up her car, then to the motel to gather her belongings. In the motel room Tina felt weak.

Joel tried to comfort her. "Tina, we have to get back home soon so you can talk to the father, ¿bueno?" he said. Tina looked at the carpet, the television, and the strange, multicolored, striped walls. "The best time I ever had in my whole life," she heard Héctor's voice echo in the room.

The drive back was difficult for Joel. He and Tina rode in silence. Tina kept looking at the ambulance. At times they would fall behind a good distance, catch up, then fall behind again. They couldn't stay with the ambulance very long because Julio drove too fast.

When they arrived in Edcouch, they went directly to the Stillman Funeral Home so Tina could make arrangements with Mr. Stillman. Judge Gómez and the priest met Tina at the funeral home, and she cried when she saw them.

The women of the church led a beautiful rosary. Our Fathers and Hail Marys were repeated with sincerity as Tina held tightly onto her rosary. She tried not to think of what was happening by focusing on the glossy, black beads, one by one.

The funeral was sad. People thought more about Tina than Héctor. "What is she going to do now?" they said. "Pobrecita."

The months after Héctor's death were not easy for Tina. She didn't talk to her co-workers as much as before, and she slowly began gaining more weight. She stopped wearing slacks and started wearing house dresses. She began calling in sick to work, sometimes taking two days off, only to sit in her house and do nothing. Finally she quit. Tina had some money in savings and her house was paid for, so she figured she could go without working for a few months, maybe even a year.

People didn't see much of Tina anymore. She didn't go to the football games nor did she attend church. The outside of her house began looking shabby. She didn't tend her flowers anymore, although Paco still mowed her lawn. A woman named Rosa began buying groceries for Tina. Tina would give Rosa two checks, one for ten dollars and the other for the groceries. Now Tina could stay in her house all the time and she did.

Tina did come out for the Easter Sunday mass, but she went to the early mass to avoid seeing people. She put on a black dress and a black veil to cover her face, and she took her rosary, the one with the black beads she knew so well.

Most people at church did not recognize Tina, and those who did were shocked. Tina had gained so much weight and her hair had turned a dark gray. Her eyes were sad eyes, not the eyes one should have on the day Christ rose from the dead. The parishioners looked colorful in their Easter Sunday clothes. The men were dressed in clean, pressed suits, and the women wore bright, flowery-print dresses, but Tina was dressed in black. She was still in mourning. All through the mass Tina could see Héctor's casket at the altar, and she cried quiet tears.

Tina was not seen again for many weeks. On the first anniversary of Héctor's death Tina spent most of the day in church. She prayed the rosary, then she just sat in the pew. When the priest walked in and passed by her, he did not know who she was at first, but then, after looking back, he realized it was Tina. She had gained more weight, and her year of mourning had aged her. He thought maybe he should talk to her, but what could he say to ease her pain? He had seen people mourn like this before. That night he prayed for Tina.

Rosa hadn't spoken to Tina in over a week, so she called Tina to see if she needed any groceries, which would give her an excuse to use the car to see a special friend. There was no answer at Tina's house. Rosa called again that night, and again there was no answer. The next day Rosa walked from her house to Tina's.

Rosa saw Tina's car in the driveway and on reaching the door could smell a stench in the air. Rosa thought, What if Tina is dead? but that only happened on television. She knocked and called out, "Tina, soy yo, Rosa. Tina?" No response. Again she called out. She slowly opened the front door and the smell overwhelmed her. Rosa gagged a little and called out, "Tina, Tina, soy yo, Rosa." Rosa began to worry. The house was warm, almost hot, because all the windows and doors were closed. There was trash everywhere. Empty cans and bottles littered the living room. The walls and the floors of the hall were streaked with brown stains, and dirty clothes lay in small piles in the hall and in the living room. Rosa was sick to her stomach from the smell of urine and waste.

She called out as she walked down the hall, knowing she would not get an answer. She passed the bathroom on the left, which smelled as bad as the house. The next door on the right was Tina's room. She opened the door, but could not get it to open all the way. Something was blocking the door. Rosa looked in and could see Tina's body lying face down parallel to the door. Tina's leg was blocking the door. "Tina, Tina," she said, but she knew the poor woman was probably dead. Rosa called the police from Tina's house and told them that she thought Tina was dead, but that they better send an ambulance just in case she wasn't.

Julio was on duty when the call came in. He drove through the dirt street fast, kicking up dust and rocks. Not because he was concerned about Tina, but because he liked driving fast and watching the dust he left behind. Rosa stood outside the house waiting when Julio drove up. He stepped out of the car slowly, adjusting his belt and dark sunglasses.

"¿Qué pasa, Rosa?" he asked.

"I'm the one who called. I think Tina is dead," she said.

"Is she inside the house?"

"Sí, she's in her room. I can show you," she said.

On entering the house Julio was hit by the smell. "Oye, apesta a mia'os," he said.

"Yeah, it's real bad," Rosa said.

Julio couldn't believe what a mess the house was. Only houses that had been abandoned for months looked like this; kids would trash the house and sometimes urinate on the walls and floors.

"Man, what the hell happened here?" he asked as they walked down the short hall to Tina's room.

"You can't open the door all the way. Her leg is in the way," Rosa said. Julio pushed on the door until he could squeeze his way into the room. Tina's room was no different from the rest of the house. He looked down at her large body. Her gray hair was stiff and looked like wire. In fact, Tina didn't look real at all but more like a bloated mannequin. Just then, he heard one of the ambulance drivers calling out.

"Julio is over here," Rosa said.

Johnny and Juan walked in with their first-aid kit. "Hey, Rosa. Where is she?" Johnny asked.

"She's in there with Julio. I think she's dead."

Johnny and Juan looked into the room.

"Come in here and help me move her away from the door," Julio said. The three men pulled Tina away from the door and turned her over. Juan felt for a pulse, though he knew she was dead.

Juan looked up at Julio and Johnny. "Está muerta," he said. "We better call the judge so he can pronounce her dead."

By now people were gathering outside. Some of the neighborhood kids were looking through the windows. Julio had to chase them away. He told the people to stay off the property. Julio called the judge from Tina's house and explained the situation. Minutes later the judge drove up and found a small crowd of people wondering what was going on. He nodded to some of them and walked inside. Seeing Tina lying on the floor stopped him for a few seconds. Tina's rosary hung to one side, and dark circles shadowed her eyelids. He looked over at Johnny and Juan.

"What did you men find?" he asked.

"She has no pulse, Judge," Juan said. "I checked. She's dead."

The judge pronounced Tina dead without question.

"Get her down to Stillman Funeral Home and don't let the people see her body," the judge said. The judge left, and the three men began to move things out of the way so they could move Tina's body.

Juan drove the ambulance closer to the front door of the house so they could put Tina's body in. He and Johnny brought down a stretcher, but she didn't fit on the narrow stretcher. Then they tried to roll her body onto a sheet to drag her out. The three men struggled to move her body out of the room, but only Tina's legs made it through the door.

"Shit, man. She's bigger than a tinaco now. And all this dead weight," Julio said. "¿Sabes qué? Let me call the fire department. Some of the guys are there and they can help us get her out."

The Edcouch fire truck drove up along with the rescue unit. They pulled up to the house without sirens but with their emergency lights on. By now more people had gathered around Tina's house, asking questions.

The four firemen talked with Julio, Johnny, and Juan about how they could get Tina out of the house. They couldn't get her out through the windows because the windows were too high and too small, and she didn't fit through her own bedroom door.

One of the firemen who came with the rescue unit looked at Tina, then at the bedroom door. "Wait, any of you ever see that movie *Animal House*? You know, the one with John Belushi?" The fireman asked. One fireman nodded, and Julio said yeah.

"Well, remember when the horse died in that office? Remember? They had to cut up the horse to get it out of the office. Well, same here, except it would be like cutting up a cow!" All the men laughed and nodded on hearing such a good, timely joke.

"Hey," the other fireman from the rescue unit spoke up. "We have a chain saw in the rescue van, and we could cut the door frame so we can get the body out." The men thought for a second or two.

"Yeah, man, it could work," Julio said. With that the men began to discuss where to cut the door frame and how much so they could get the body out. One of the firemen went out to the rescue van to get the chain saw. When the people saw this, they became really curious.

"¿Oye, que van a hacer con eso?" The fireman answered, "Nada."

The men marked where to cut, and the gas-powered chain saw was turned on. The saw could easily be heard in the street, and people looked at each other not sure what to think.

Tina's body was moved two feet away from the door, and one of the men cut through the frame and wall. Dust and chips of wood and paint spewed from the wall, slowly covering up Tina's dress and body. When the chain saw began cutting through sheetrock, a fine, white dust settled over her body, enveloping it in a cloud of powder.

The men cut the door frame on both sides until they knew that Tina could be lifted or dragged out. They cursed up and down the hall as they pulled and dragged her body down the short hall, all the while complaining about the smell coming from Tina's heavy, dead body. When they reached the front door, they found that Tina's body would not fit through the door. Again the chain saw was started.

People could see Tina's body just inside the doorway. Her feet were bare, and her brown legs and arms were covered with white dust. Again the chain saw threw dust into the air. Tina's house again slowly covered up her body.

Finally the men were able to get Tina out and heaved her into the ambulance. The people could see that the men were not gentle with Tina's body, but she was dead and they could tell she was heavy. The ambulance driver turned on the lights and drove away through the dirt streets.

The next night the Stillman Funeral Home held a closed-casket rosary for Tina. Tina's supervisor from work wanted to say a few words, but Judge Gómez felt he should be the one to say something. The pews filled up with the townspeople, most of whom were not sure why they were there. The judge was not sure what he was going to say. He stood there and looked at the people, who were wondering what he was going to say.

"Everyone here knew Tina. She was a good woman, who liked going to football games and church bingos. She was just like all of us here. Tina also had a son, Héctor, and like all of us here who have hijos and hijas . . . Well, we love our kids, eh? When Tina came to me to adopt Héctor, she was pretty nervous, and when I signed the papers making her Héctor's legal guardian, she was very happy.

"I know Tina is happy now because she is with Héctor. That is why she died, to be with him. None of us wants to be alone in this world or up there in Heaven, even though there are angels and God. I am glad you came tonight. Let's pray for Tina and Héctor to be happy." Judge Gómez wasn't sure if what he had said was good or not, but some people cried nonetheless.

The funeral was held the next morning because the Valley sun would get very hot in the afternoon. Tina was buried next to Héctor. The judge attended the funeral, as well as Rosa and a couple of Tina's former co-workers. As Tina was lowered into the ground no tears were shed.

At Tina's house Julio and Joel walked around making a list of the valuables. Judge Gómez wanted to know what could be salvaged and given to the church. Joel couldn't believe it smelled as bad as Julio had described it. Empty tin cans, dirty clothes, tissue papers, and cans of dust cleaner were scattered throughout the house. Julio picked up one of the cans of dust cleaner and noticed it was empty. He picked up another and it, too was empty. He found another and that, too, was empty. They were all empty. With all these empty cans of dust cleaner you would think her furniture would be clean, he thought to himself.

"Man, this woman lived like a pig. Look at all this," Julio said.

"There was something wrong with her. I mean, it must have been because her kid died or something," Joel said.

"That doesn't mean you should turn into a pig or at least not as big as one," said Julio.

"Come on, man. The poor woman is dead."

"Poor, my ass. You didn't have to get her fat, dead body out of here," Julio said. "I mean, look, man, we had to cut down half the door to get her out. This woman was crazy. I mean, look at this house. It looks like shit. She didn't care about anything. You would think she might at least clean the kitchen or her own bedroom, man."

Joel nodded. Walking down the hall past Tina's bedroom, he came to a locked door. He turned the knob a few times and pushed, but the door wouldn't open.

"Hey, Julio. This door is locked. What do you think?" Joel said.

"I don't know, man. It's probably full of shit or something," he laughed. "You open it and you clean it." Together they broke the door open.

It was Héctor's room. The brothers stood in the center of the room. Héctor's bed was made with straight, folded edges. Julio opened the closet door, and there were Héctor's clothes hanging neatly on hangers. His shoes were paired up and in a straight row. No dust on his shoes. On the wall were posters of the Houston Astros baseball team and a black-and-gold Edcouch-Elsa high-school pennant. Against the wall by the window was Héctor's dresser, looking shiny and new. On the dresser was a photograph in a blue frame. It was the photograph of Tina and Héctor at Astroworld, their arms in the air as if on a roller coaster, laughing.

The Barcos didn't say a word for a few seconds. Then Julio looked over at Joel.

"Know why this room is so clean?"

Joel shook his head slowly.

"Because the door was locked. If Tina la Tinaca had gotten in here, it would be a mess, too."

Empty Corner

The quick jab to his jaw rattled his brain. It felt as if his eyes were spinning in their sockets as his mouthpiece shot out, covered in saliva and blood. Coach Garza, standing outside the corner of the ring, knew this would happen. Marcos just couldn't help picking on a smaller fighter, especially one who did not like to fight.

"That's enough, Marcos. Alex, you all right?"

Coach Garza knelt beside Alex, trying to help him up. Alex didn't even know he was on the canvas, but there he was, looking up at the Coach.

"You all right? Feel okay?"

"Ah, Coach! He's just being a baby. I barely hit him," Marcos said.

"Like hell, Marcos! I told you to go easy and to spar with him, not to fight him!"

"He's just being a baby, Coach," Marcos repeated.

Coach didn't have much patience, and Marcos didn't understand reasoning very well, so Coach Garza used what Marcos understood best, aggression. The coach stood up to his full six feet and walked over to Marcos's five-foot-ten frame.

"Okay, Marcos, you want to spar with me like you sparred with Alex? Do you?

Because if you want, I'll get my gloves on right now and we'll go a couple of rounds, and I'll spar with you just like you sparred with Alex."

Marcos stood silent, not making much eye contact with Coach Garza, just like a dog when it's being scolded by its master.

"Yeah, Coach, but you're bigger than me and stronger . . ."

Coach Garza shook his head. It seemed Marcos always had an excuse.

"Marcos, shut up! Go hit the showers," Coach said.

Coach Garza stared at Marcos until Marcos disappeared down the hall. Alex was sitting up now but still felt a little lightheaded. His eyes had stopped spinning, and the gym was now upright. Coach Garza extended his hand and helped Alex up.

"You're going to be okay. You just got a small cut on your lip," Coach said.

Alex got up and felt a little better. At least the coach didn't yell at him or call him some name for falling down.

"Thanks, Coach. I feel better."

"You sure you're okay?"

"Yeah, yeah, I feel better," Alex said.

"Bueno, hit the showers," Coach said.

He didn't feel better, though. He was still a little dizzy from the blow Marcos had given him, and he just wanted to go home. He walked slowly to the showers, hoping that Marcos would not be there, but there he was, already dressed to go and waiting for Alex. Alex hated confronting Marcos. Marcos stood up as Alex entered the locker room, his chest out and fist clinched. Marcos looked mean and he knew that he scared Alex. He walked up to Alex just as Coach Garza had done to him earlier.

"Pinche güey. You're lucky the Coach is here to save your ass, but if I see you on the street or . . ."

Suddenly Coach Garza appeared at the entrance.

"If you see Alex on the street, what are you going to do, Marcos, eh? What? I'll tell you what you're going to do—nothing! You understand? Because if you bother Alex outside the gym and I hear about it, I'll tell your parents that you can't come here anymore, and I won't train you anymore. You understand that, Marcos? Do you?" Coach asked.

Once again Marcos became the obedient dog and said nothing.

"Do you understand? Yes or no?" Coach demanded.

"Yeah, Coach," Marcos answered.

"No, Marcos. Yes or no," Coach said.

"Yes, Coach."

"Yes, what?"

"Yes, I understand, Coach."

Coach Garza stood still staring at Marcos, his chest raised and both hands on his hips.

"Bueno. Now go home, and we'll see you tomorrow at four-thirty on the dot," Coach said.

Coach Garza had saved Alex for the hundredth time this month, and Alex hadn't even fought in a real fight yet.

Coach Garza liked Alex. Alex was smart, not stupid like Marcos. Coach Garza had had high hopes for Marcos at one time, but he turned out to be a stupid bully like others he had trained before. Alex, though, could be a good fighter, maybe even a great fighter. Alex was a southpaw, and Coach knew he could train Alex to win fights. It would just take some time and a little patience. But one thing was certain: Coach Garza was going to make a fighter out of him, one way or another.

"Bueno, Alex, hit the showers and don't worry about Marcos. He's just jealous because he knows one day you'll be a great boxer and he won't amount to nothing," Coach said with a slight nod.

Alex felt better knowing Coach was there to help him with Marcos. And it felt good to know that Coach believed in him. But Alex knew he would never be a great boxer. He had never wanted to be a boxer; it was his father's idea. Alex had told his father he didn't like boxing, but his father wouldn't listen. His father would tell Alex to be a man and not act like his sisters.

As the hot water flowed over Alex's fourteen-year-old body, he relaxed. The water stung the open wound on his lip, and his head still echoed from the jab, but at least he was out of the ring. Two months had passed and he still did not like boxing. His stomach growled as he thought about his mother's cooking and wondered what she might have to eat at home.

Alex's house was warm with the aroma of Spanish rice, beans, and tortillas. His mother tended to the cooking, and his three sisters set the table. The women flowed from table to stove in a dance that neither Alex nor his father had learned. Whenever Alex or his father wandered into the kitchen, they would only step on feet and trip the women's dance.

Once everyone was seated and served, the family would begin a discussion that would eventually end up in a dispute. Verónica, the oldest sister, like everyone else at the table, noticed Alex's swollen lip.

"Alejandro, what happened to your lip?" Verónica asked.

Alex took a deep breath and began to utter the first word in his sentence, but the sound was drowned out by his father.

"¡Nada pasó! It's just a little cut. Boxers get cuts on the lip all the time," his father said.

"Well, that's pretty big for a little cut," Verónica replied.

Verónica was the one in college and was considered the smartest one in the family. She knew Alex didn't like boxing and would try to protect Alex from her father's machismo.

"What? You can hardly see it," the father said.

"Well, at least you didn't get a black eye or a broken jaw," María said, the baby of the family. "Who punched you?"

"Marcos did," Alex said.

"Marcos! Marcos is a jerk and a bully and ugly. Nobody at school likes him," Suzanna said, making a face of disgust.

"One day, Alex, you'll be big enough to beat him up," María said with music in her voice.

Alex began to smile, but he could feel his lip open, and the salt from the hot rice stung.

"Well, he'll never beat up anybody if he doesn't take his boxing seriously," his father said.

"Well, maybe he shouldn't be taking boxing lessons," Verónica said. "I mean, Alex doesn't even like boxing, and what good is it anyway? Right, Alex?"

Alex said nothing; he just looked at the white table-cloth. It covered the table in a flower pattern filled with holes. He could see the bare, brown table underneath, thinking of how crumbs always managed to get under the tablecloth.

"Tell him, Alex," Verónica urged him.

"Verónica, would you let your brother talk for once!" Alex's father snapped. "You're always interrupting everybody. You never let anybody talk. Now, Alex, is it true you want to quit?"

Alex looked at Verónica, who nodded slightly as if to say, Go on. Then he looked at his other two sisters, who were afraid Alex was going to say that he didn't want to box anymore. Then there was his mother, who looked tired of the whole affair. Alex looked at his father.

The room became the ring he hated. In this corner of the table sat the challenger, Alex. Weighing in at 120 pounds and holding no titles. And in that corner sat the undefeated champion, Alex's father. Weighing in at 165 pounds; his father, the man of the house and king of the castle.

"Yeah, Dad, I don't want to box anymore," Alex said.

"What! Why not? Coach Garza says you're getting better all the time, and he thinks you can be a great fighter," his father said. "Is Marcos bothering you? Because if he is, I'll talk to Coach Garza and he'll straighten him out."

Alex thought for a moment that he could use Marcos as an excuse, but knew it would just cause more problems.

"No, no one is bothering me," he said, shaking his head. "I just don't like it. I'd rather play soccer or something else."

"You don't like it! Well, you're not going to like it when someone beats you up!" his father burst out. "How's soccer going to help you in a fight? Eh?"

Alex's mother, the only person who could silence her husband, finally spoke.

"¡Ya! Por favor, Roberto, ¡déjalo!" she said in a raised voice as if she were scolding one of the children. "If he doesn't want to box then he doesn't have to! Si quieres, *you* take boxing lessons."

The family was silent for a second, then Alex's father spoke.

"You do what you want. Pero when you get into a fight and get beat up, don't come crying to me." With that, Alex's father got up and left the room. The rest of the family sat in silence looking at each other and in unison exhaled in relief. "¡Ese hombre!" Alex's mother said in frustration.

"Why is he that way? He's always getting mad about something," Verónica said. "Well, Alex, it looks like you finally won one."

Alex said nothing. He nodded slowly as if to agree with Verónica, but he didn't know that this was just round one.

The following day Alex was a little happier knowing he didn't have to box. After school he walked home with some stride in his step. He watched television trying to find something he liked. Alex looked at the clock on the wall showing the time was four-thirty. Right at this time, if he were still in training, he would be stretching so he could begin doing push-ups and sit-ups until it hurt. Alex was happy he wasn't at the gym. Just then the phone rang. He answered it, recognizing the voice almost immediately. It was Coach Garza.

"Hey, Alex, it's four-thirty. Why aren't you here?" he asked.

"Hey, Coach, uh . . . well, you see, I don't want to box anymore, Coach."

"Now listen, Alex, your father called me last night and told me you didn't want to train anymore, and I think I know why," Coach said. "It's Marcos, right?"

"No, Coach, it's . . ."

"Look, Alex, I know he likes to pick on you, but he won't be picking on you anymore, okay? I told Marcos he'll have to find another trainer, so it'll be just you and me from now on. What do you say?"

Alex was glad that Coach wasn't mad at him, but he just didn't want to train anymore. How was he going to tell Coach without making him mad, especially after all his patience and now getting rid of Marcos, too?

"Come on, Alex. You're almost there," Coach continued.

"Maybe later, Coach. Next year or something, but I just need some time off to think about it, you know?"

"Alex, the more time you take off, the more out of shape you'll get, and it'll be twice as hard to get you back into shape," Coach said. "And besides, boxing will keep you in shape for soccer when the season starts."

Alex again thought for a moment. "Coach, let me think about it . . ."

"Listen, Alex, boxing can also help you in a fight," Coach continued.

"I know, Coach, I know, but if you can just give me some time, okay?"

"All right, Alex, I'll give you some time to think about it, but when you are ready just let me know, okay?"

"Thanks, Coach."

Alex was glad that was over. Now he could go on with other things and not worry about boxing.

The following weeks were good for Alex. His father was speaking to him and not making as many comments as before. Comments such as: "Since you aren't doing anything now, why don't you help your sisters in the kitchen" or "Did you get into a fight today? Because when you do, you'll see."

One afternoon Alex stayed late at school so he could attend a soccer club meeting. His father said he would pick him up around five-thirty. The meeting was over at five o'clock, and Alex sat on the steps of the school waiting. At five-thirty his father had not shown up yet, but it was typical for him to be late. He called home and no one answered. At six o'clock Alex assumed that his father had forgotten, and not wanting to wait, he began walking home.

Alex walked home thinking about soccer, and every now and then kicked a can or a rock with the side of his foot. He stopped at a store to call home, but again there was no answer.

It was starting to get dark, and Alex could see the fluorescent lights in the shopping centers and gas stations. All he needed was to pass one more convenience store, and then he would be in his neighborhood, only a few blocks from home.

As he passed the dumpster of the convenience store, he felt a hard slap on his right arm and then a quick, tight grip. Before Alex could look at his attacker, he was jerked behind the dumpster and hit square in the face. One hard blow followed another and another. The punches made him see bright electrical storms flashing through his brain. Who could this be . . . Marcos? He thought for a second. Alex tried to wrap his arms around the person just as he would do in training, but when he did, he received a blow to his stomach. Alex gasped for air as he began to fall, but the person was strong and wouldn't let Alex hit the ground, holding him up for another hit that finally made him drop to the pavement.

Alex opened his eyes and saw the headlights of a car shining on him, and someone was trying to talk to him. He knew he was hurt because his face was numb, and it was difficult for him to keep his eyes open. The person asked questions: "You all right? Can you talk? What's your name and where do you live?" Alex slowly sat up with the woman's help; she sounded like his sister, but she wasn't. All he could tell was that she had dark hair and was wearing jeans. He wiped his mouth on his shirt, and the blood looked black under the yellow street lamps.

Alex told her that he didn't live far from the store and asked if she would give him a ride home. When they arrived at Alex's home, he tried to thank her and tell her that he could make it just fine from there, but the words were not coming out and the numbness was wearing off and the pain was beginning to pulsate.

She walked him to the front door and rang the doorbell. Alex kept his head down and lightly leaned on the woman. His mother answered the doorbell. Alex looked up at her.

"Ay Dios, Alejandro. ¿Qué te pasó?" she said as the blood rushed from her face.

Alex said nothing; he only sighed, trying to figure out how he was going to explain what he didn't understand.

"Someone was attacking him or something at the store down the street," said the woman who was with him. "I didn't get to see him really. He ran off when I drove up."

Now all four women were at the door, taking Alex and the woman into the house; they gathered around him, each of them having some physical contact with him.

"What happened, now?" Verónica asked, as if she were the official historian of the family. The woman explained how she had seen a man attacking Alex at the store, and that he ran off when she drove up.

"Did you get a good look at him?" Verónica asked.

"No, it was dark and he was already running away as I drove up."

As she finished speaking, the headlights of a car flashed across Alex's house. His father's car pulled into the driveway. He knew what his father was going to say, as did the women of the house. They all paused and looked at the headlights and heard the engine shut off.

"Great. That's all we need," Verónica said.

The woman who brought Alex could sense the tension building. She knew that something was about to start, and she didn't want to be there when it did.

"Ah, if you will excuse me, uhm . . . I really need to be going."

Alex's mother quickly smiled at her and thanked her.

"Thank you for all that you have done. You have been very kind," she said with a polite smile as she walked the woman out. The woman took the thank-you and left quickly.

Alex's head throbbed and it hurt so much that all he could hear was a sharp ringing sound. His sisters laid him down on the sofa, and one of them wiped his cuts and bruises with a warm cloth. His father came into the house and knew something had happened.

"Who was that woman? What's going on here, eh?"

Alex's mother looked at him, knowing that there was no easy way to tell him what had happened to Alex. Then out of nowhere Verónica spoke up.

"Someone beat him up! So there! Are you happy now?" She said as if he were to blame. "That's what you wanted, right? So he would have to take those damn boxing lessons again. Right?"

"Well, he would have been fine if he was still boxing. This never would have happened," her father shouted. "See, I told you this would happen. But not one of you would listen. Especially you, Verónica, and now your brother has been beaten up because of you!"

"¡Ya, Roberto! ¿Por qué eres así? Your son is hurt! He doesn't need to hear your lectures now," Alex's mother said in defense and in anger.

Alex felt like crying but he couldn't because he was mad at himself and mad that his father was right.

"Ya, that's enough. I just want to go to my room. Please, I can take care of myself," Alex said as he began to get up. He kept looking down, not wanting his family to see his face. Alex's mother put her hand to his chin and lifted it slightly. She noticed that his lips were cut in two places and his eyes were swelling. She felt terrible for Alex. "Ay, m'hijo," she said.

Alex's mother and sisters surrounded him with soft voices as Alex walked towards his room. María had tears in her eyes, and Suzanna put her arm around María's shoulder to keep her from crying. The wife glanced at her husband with hate as she walked her son away.

Alex's father stood alone in the room listening to the voices fade. He felt that maybe he should say something kind to Alex but instead walked into the kitchen, took a beer out of the refrigerator, twisted off the cap, and took a drink. The coolness of the bottle and the taste of the beer soothed his racing blood. He took another drink, then reached for the telephone to dial the number he'd been dialing so often the week before. An answering machine came on.

"Hello, this is Ron Garza, thanks for calling but I'm not home right now. But if you leave a message and a phone number at the sound of the beep, I'll get back to you as soon as I can."

The beep sounded for a few seconds. "Hello, Coach Garza, this is Roberto Reyes, Alex's father. I think your idea worked. Maybe Alex will start training again next week. Don't call me, I'll call you."

He hung up the telephone and took another drink. He sat down on a chair and rubbed his knuckles, wondering if his son would ever know how much he loved him.

In the Canal

Pete's boss shook his head, and his right fist slammed the kitchen table. His breakfast plate of chorizo con huevos and fork rattled.

"You did what? How the hell can you lose an arm?"

Pete was afraid. He could see the mad blood turning Cheto's brown face a dark red. This was what Cheto looked like before killing someone.

"I think it's in the canal," Pete quickly replied, trying to reassure his boss.

"Well, you better find it before somebody else does," Cheto said. "And you better hope no one finds the damn body."

"No problem, Cheto, I'll make sure everything is taken care of," Pete said, trying again to reassure his boss.

"Hell, you better or your *head* will be missing," Cheto threatened. "Go and get it and take Steve with you."

"But they were primos."

"¿Y qué? You mean Steve doesn't have any other cousins?" Cheto asked, giving him no time for a reply. "Listen, pendejo, if pinche Ricky was an informant, then maybe Steve is also an informant. If he makes a big deal about Ricky or asks a lot of fucking questions, kill the motherfucker. Ya vete, and, Pete, don't fuck it up because if you do, your cousins will wonder what happened to *you*."

Pete could see that Cheto wasn't in the mood for mistakes and understood all too well what happens to fuckups.

Sitting in his truck, he thought that he shouldn't have chopped off Ricky's arm, but he wanted to look cool in front of the other men. Sure, Ricky deserved it. After all, he was giving information to the police, but he shouldn't have chopped off his arm. "Gotta learn to control my temper," he said to himself as he pulled into the parking lot of a convenience store to call Steve.

Pete called Steve to tell him they had to do something. Steve was getting used to hearing the word "something," which could mean anything. It could mean picking up some stuff close to the border or taking some stuff to someone somewhere, anywhere. Once, "something" meant picking up some new furniture for the boss. He had been working for Cheto only a few weeks, and the money was good, and Cheto seemed to like him.

Pete drove his truck through the streets of Edcouch in no hurry, trying to blend in with the other cars on the road, even though everybody in town knew who was driving the bright green truck with the dark-tinted windows.

In his mind he went over what he might have to say to Steve about Ricky. It crossed his mind that Steve might also be an informant, and he thought how he would kill him and where. Shit! And what if one of the farmers found the damn arm or if it sank or something. Fish! Fish could have eaten the fucking arm. His mind spun with the possibilities.

Steve found that weekends were hard on his body. Drinking, smoking, and dancing till two in the morning, every weekend, were catching up with his twenty-two-year-old body. Not even the football games he had played in high school had made him feel this bad. He heard the rumble of Pete's truck coming down the street and hoped that whatever Cheto needed wouldn't take long.

Steve got into the truck, and they shook hands in the way most male friends in the Valley did. Steve knew not to talk until Pete did, even though Pete was not much older, but he had been working with Cheto even before Cheto was paralyzed, so Pete had been around and seen more.

Steve had heard stories of how Cheto and Pete were once set up and almost killed, but that Pete saved Cheto's life. It was said that Pete killed all the other guys, even though they were outnumbered and outgunned.

"We're going over to Mile 18 to one of the canals to pick up something," Pete said without looking over at Steve.

The irrigation canals were made of long, narrow cement troughs running along the fields. It seemed that every field had a canal running along it, and the canal banks were the closest thing to what could be called a hill. Walls of dirt six feet high and twenty feet wide. High enough to see the fields and wide enough to drive a truck on.

At night the kids of the town would come to these canals to drink beer, smoke, have sex, and sometimes settle their differences. During the day younger kids would come to the canals to shoot their BB guns and ride their bikes.

On this Saturday morning, as on every other Saturday morning, a group of boys from Edcouch had come to ride their bikes on the canal banks. They had gotten up early and packed some lunch and filled their canteens with water. It was a two-mile ride to the canals from town.

They rode in the middle of the empty farm roads, zigzagging around the yellow lines, playing follow-the-leader. One rode on the white line of the shoulder and the others followed. Once they got there, they rode up and down the canals and raced each other down into the fields.

Mark, the one in high school, was the oldest of the four boys and challenged the others to a BB gun shooting contest. Each of the boys gathered up empty beer cans and bottles and lined them up for target practice. Mark and Frankie went up one canal and Joe and René went up the other. Targets littered the canals, especially after a Friday night.

Frankie began picking up cans, but Mark kept an eye out for beer bottles. In the dark canal water Mark saw what he thought was a big stick or maybe a snake. He hoped it was a snake so they could shoot it.

"Frankie! Come here! I think I found a snake."

Frankie looked up, and so did Joe and René.

"Come on! Mark found a snake!" Joe said to René. Both jumped on their bikes and rode over to Mark and Frankie.

Mark went down on one knee to get a closer look; he then realized it wasn't a snake but something else.

"What do you think it is?" Frankie asked. "Could it be a dead snake or something dead?"

Joe and René rode their bikes up the canal and jumped off.

"Be careful, Mark, it could be a water moccasin or a cottonmouth," Joe said.

All the boys bent down and looked at the strange floating object. Slowly each began to realize that it wasn't a stick or a snake. Mark could see fingers and the gleam of a silver watch and fine black hairs swaying with the lifeless rhythm of the canal water.

"Shit. It's an arm!" Mark said in a scared tone. Following Mark's instructions, the boys began looking for sticks so they could get the arm out. After a few minutes and several tries, they managed to get it out. They could see the bone and dark red flesh at the end of the arm. Each made a face of disgust. Mark knelt to take a closer look at the watch on the arm. He had seen that watch before.

Pete could see the boys up on the canal bank and had a terrible feeling that they'd found the arm. That was all he needed. He thought that he could scare the kids away or pay them something to keep their mouths shut.

The green truck came to a smooth stop, and the rumbling engine fell silent. The boys knew the truck and they began to worry.

"Mark, let's get out of here," Joe said, knowing the green truck meant trouble.

. Frankie and René didn't wait for Mark's answer; they got on their bikes, but before they could begin to pedal, Pete got out of the truck. His black felt cowboy hat shielded his face from the morning sun. On the other side of the truck, Steve got out and quickly recognized his cousin Mark.

"Hold on! You guys wait right there," Pete said in a serious and threatening voice. The boys didn't move; they had a bad feeling, but Mark wasn't afraid because his cousin Steve was with Pete. Mark said in a quiet voice to the others, "Don't worry, that's my cousin Steve. It'll be okay."

Pete walked up the canal bank with Steve following close behind. When he got to the top, Pete could see the arm lying on the ground behind the boys, and he knew that he had to control the situation fast.

"Get on your bikes and get out of here," Pete said in a calm voice so as not to get the boys too scared. Joe, René, and Frankie proceeded to mount their bikes, but Mark's voice froze them.

"Not until you tell us whose arm that is," Mark said in a demanding voice.

Pete was not about to let this kid show him up, so he pointed to Mark in a rude, condescending manner.

"None of your fucking business. Now I'm going to tell you one more time. All of you get on your fucking bikes and get out of here!"

Mark didn't move. Frankie looked over at him. "Come on, Mark, let's go."

Steve knew that Mark could be a little stubborn at times.

"Mark, you and your friends better go. We're not playing around here," Steve said trying to ease the mounting tension.

Again Mark didn't move, and Frankie pleaded with Mark again, "Come on, Mark, let's get out of here."

Mark looked past Pete directly into Steve's eyes.

"Not until my cousin Steve tells me why my brother's arm is here."

Steve's eyes showed surprise, and Pete knew he had lost control of the situation.

"What are you talking about?" Steve shouted.

"That's Ricky's watch!" Mark pointed to the limb. "I know it is, because we gave it to him for graduation."

Pete began wondering what he could do to get out of this mess. He looked over at Steve, who looked as if he wanted some kind of answer. Steve started walking towards the severed arm.

"Look, I don't have time to explain nothing! Just tell your fucking cousin and his stupid friends to get out of here," Pete said. "Don't get them involved in this."

"I am already involved," Mark said with confidence in his voice, now that Steve seemed to be on his side of the argument. Mark's friends began to move slowly away from Mark.

"Look, you little smart-ass. . . . You little shits stay where you are!"

Steve could now clearly see the watch on the brown arm. It was Ricky's watch on the dead arm. Steve could hear Pete yelling at Mark.

"Shit, man! Where the hell is my cousin?" Steve demanded. "Pete! Where is he, man? What did you do to him?"

Pete was not sure what to do. All those witnesses, and now Steve was against him. It was bad shit. He snapped the buttons on his black Western shirt and pulled out his nickel-plated Colt 45. So quick was his draw that Steve and the boys were stunned. They simply looked at the black hole surrounded by polished nickel.

"Hey, man, put that . . ." Steve began, but was cut off immediately.

"Shut the fuck up, Steve. If your stupid, little, fucking cousin kept his mouth shut, this wouldn't have to happen," Pete said with determined anger. "But no, the little shit is stupid just like Ricky was." Pete's eyes burned into Mark's eyes. "I told you and your fucking friends to get out of here, but you wouldn't listen."

Steve knew that Pete had a way of breaking what he couldn't fix. Steve could feel his pistol burning at the small of his back. Could he reach for it before Pete would begin his killing?

Joe began to cry and begged in a broken voice, "Please, don't shoot us. We promise we won't . . ."

Pete pointed the pistol at the sobbing boy. "Shut the fuck up!"

In that one moment, Steve reached for his gun with a quick movement like he'd seen on all the cop shows, but he failed to grab the pistol and in his hurried panic jammed it down his jeans.

Pete needed Steve to do something stupid so he could feel better about killing him. Pete didn't panic and fired his Colt 45. The bullet cut through Steve's chest, throwing him backward. Mark stood still, hoping Pete would not fire, but Pete shot him below the neck. Mark made a horrid groaning sound and fell into the canal, breaking the dark water.

Joe, Frankie, and René began screaming and crying in high-pitched sounds, screaming like babies for their mothers. Their pleas were cut short by loud gunfire. Pete's eyes watched each of the boys' bodies explode into flesh and blood as his bullets ripped through their innocence. Suddenly, all was calm. Only a bicycle wheel moved. Round and round.

Pete put his gun down and let his lungs exhale. "Shit," was his first word. He looked around and across at the highway and could see no one. He could feel a sense of panic but tried to get his head straight. "Okay, okay, okay, think," he said to himself. He could see the dead bodies scattered in front of him in unnatural positions. Arms and legs all pointed in different directions. Mark's body floated in the red-stained canal water, and that gave Pete an idea.

He shoved his gun back in his jeans and grabbed the boy closest to him. He dragged the light body to edge of the canal bank, then pushed it in with his boot. The limp body rolled into the canal and floated face up. Pete moved quickly. One by one he dragged and kicked each body into the red canal. After all five bodies were in the water, he threw bicycles in on top of the floating bodies.

Pete stood still for a second and tried to catch his breath. He looked around to make sure he hadn't forgotten anything. He began to walk towards his truck and then suddenly remembered the arm.

There the arm laid looking slimy and milky with flies hovering over it. Pete rushed over and stared at it for a moment. He could still hear Ricky screaming and the other guys laughing.

He reached down, grabbed the arm by the wrist, hurried to his truck, and threw the arm into the bed of the truck. Then he jumped in, turned on his loud engine, and sped down the highway towards Edcouch.

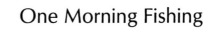
One Morning Fishing

It's not easy being a father. A father has to compete with other fathers as in "My daddy is bigger than your daddy." "Oh yeah? Well, my daddy can beat up your daddy." Fathers can usually compete with other fathers, but to compete against Ward Cleaver, Dr. Alex Stone, and all-time champion Andy Taylor is sometimes too much.

When I was eight years old, my father took my younger brother Roger and me fishing mainly because Andy Taylor took Opie fishing. Dad did everything he could to be a good father. He showed interest in every-thing my brother and I did. We joined the Boy Scouts; Dad joined the Boy Scouts. We became junior volunteer firemen; Dad became a volunteer fireman. Whatever sport we played in high school, Dad would attend all the games and cheer regardless of how much time we spent on the bench. So when Roger and I wanted to go fish-ing, Dad took us fishing.

On Saturday morning Roger and I were up early so we could watch the best cartoons. It was about a quarter to eight when Dad told us we had to leave soon to get a good fishing spot. Dad didn't own any fishing equipment, so we had to buy all our fishing gear first thing in the morning. He got Mom up so she could make some tacos for us to eat. Mom made extra tacos and wrapped them in foil paper for us to eat later, and she packed some Hunt's snack-pack pudding. With our lunches and a jug of water we were ready to go fishing. Roger and I hopped into Dad's yellow Ford Galaxy 500, and off we went to Delta Lake.

It was a man-made lake just past a small town called Monte Alto about fifteen miles from our hometown of Edcouch. Delta Lake wasn't deep blue or transparent gray like lakes on postcards. It was a murky dark green with patches of brown here and there. Some of the trees submerged in the water could still be seen. Their dead, bare branches were gray and black and looked like the fingers of unseen hands. Attempting to water-ski on Delta Lake would be stupid because of the trees, but then nobody skied on the lake because nobody owned a ski boat.

It was a scary lake. Over twelve people had drowned in it, with one death caused by some mysterious amoeba. There were big, white signs all around the lake with red letters: Danger. Swimming Is Not Allowed in Delta Lake. This warning was written in English and Spanish. To top it off, the sign also had an illustration of a skull and crossbones like the kind seen on bottles containing poison. I doubt that Delta Lake is on any postcards. It wasn't the best of lakes, but it was all we had. Besides, we weren't planning to eat the fish we caught. None of us liked fish or, for that matter, any other type of seafood.

On the way to Delta Lake, Dad played his favorite eight-track tape, the Credence Clearwater Revival. It was CCR's greatest hits, and Roger and I loved to sing along. Our favorite was "Out My Back Door," which was about animals playing in a band. One of the lines went like this: "Tambourines and elephants are playing in the band . . ." but Roger and I always said, "Tangerines and elephants are playing in the band . . ." Every time we sang that line wrong, which was every time Dad played it, he would laugh and correct us, but we would just do it again.

Once we got to the lake we stopped at the only store there, Delta Lake store, but it was closed and didn't open until nine o'clock, so we drove around the lake to see if there were any good fishing spots left. Delta Lake was surrounded by a gravel road just wide enough for two cars to pass each other. As we drove, we could see lots of fishing spots since there was no one else around. Halfway around the lake, I asked Dad if I could eat my Hunt's snack-pack pudding, but before Dad could respond to my question, Roger added, "Yeah, Dad, can we eat our pudding, please?"

"If you eat your pudding now you won't have any when you eat your lunch," Dad said.

"Ah, come on, Dad, please," I said, giving him my best puppy-eyes look. Roger looked even more puppy-eyed than I did. Roger and I never worked on anything together unless there was a strong incentive, and food like chocolate pudding always brought our stomachs together. By the time we had circled the lake once the Delta Lake store was open.

As we entered, the man sitting behind a glass counter, who was reading some kind of gun magazine, said, "Mornin'." He was an older white man and wore a white cap and red suspenders. He sat in one of those aluminum-frame lawn chairs.

The glass counter in front of him was filled with half-empty boxes of chocolate bars, gum, candy, and fishing hooks. One of the walls was covered with fishing poles and with baseball caps of all sizes and colors. On the opposite wall were refrigerator cases full of soda and beer.

In the center, the store was divided by a shelf with cookies, chips, cans of food, and toilet paper. A fine layer of dust covered everything in the store. There were Zebco fishing poles wrapped in plastic, ready to use. They were $12.99 each and came in two tones, blue and gray.

We also bought some little, gray weights and red and white cone-shaped floaters. I guess they were called floaters. Anyway, we needed some bait, and there were all types of live and dead slimy-looking bait. The man behind the counter asked Dad what kind of bait he wanted, but Dad was not sure.

"What kind of bait works best out here?" Dad asked.

"That depends. What ya fishing for?" the man said, slightly lifting his cap. Dad shrugged his shoulders.

"I don't know. What . . ."

"Catfish, Dad," Roger shouted.

"Roger!" Dad snapped, then regained his composure. "Ah yeah. We want to catch some catfish," Dad said in his best confident voice, but the man didn't look impressed. The man pointed to some red, wormy-looking bait and said that was what catfish liked best. So Dad bought half a pound of the red worms and some shrimp as well, but before we left the store, we convinced Dad to buy us some cokes and Hershey chocolate bars. We were now set to catch the biggest catfish alive in Delta Lake.

Dad found the perfect fishing spot, and we were the only people around as far as the eye could see. Alone, there on the lake, just Dad, Roger, and me.

It took some time to get our fishing poles ready since none of us really knew how to fish. Roger and I didn't want to touch the worms because they were covered with blood, but Dad said worms didn't have blood. Dad tried to get the worms on the hooks, but they kept falling off.

So he decided to use the shrimp because they were easier to stab. Roger and I didn't mind touching the shrimp, because we couldn't see any blood on them. We cast out our lines and waited for the fish to start biting. Dad left the stereo on in the car and opened the doors so we could listen to CCR while we fished.

After sitting in the Valley morning sun for about five minutes, the brotherly bond formed by the chocolate bars and pudding was dissolving fast.

"Dad, do fish bite?" Roger asked, but before Dad could answer, I said, "Fish don't bite, sonso."

"Sharks bite and killer whales do, too," Roger fired back.

"Yeah, well, there aren't any sharks and killer whales in Delta Lake, sonso!"

"That's enough from both of you, and don't call your brother a sonso," Dad said.

"Yeah, but . . ."

"David, be quiet! You're going to scare the fish away if you keep talking."

"How can they hear us? They're under water," I said.

"I didn't know fish had ears," Roger said.

"Both of you be quiet. You're going to scare the fish away if you keep making noise."

"But, Dad, you have the radio on and it's louder than us," I said.

By now Dad was irritated. "David! Roger! Listen. Just reel in your lines to see if you caught anything."

So we reeled in our lines to find nothing. We hadn't caught anything, and both our shrimps were missing. Dad said the shrimps were missing because they fell off. So we put some more bait on our hooks and tried again. Each time we reeled in our lines to see if we had caught any fish, the shrimps were gone. Each time we put the shrimps back on the hook we would try a different method of baiting the hook, but we still kept losing our shrimps. After twenty minutes of losing our shrimps, we finally lost our desire to catch the big one.

"Dad, can we go home now?" Roger asked.

"Yeah, Dad, I am ready, too. Besides, we don't even like fish."

Looking back now, I realize Dad couldn't wait to hear those words come out of our mouths.

"Are you sure? We still have lots of bait left, and it's not even lunchtime."

All we could do was nod yes.

"Okay, then. Reel in you fishing lines so we can go.

We reeled in our baitless lines, and Dad threw the red worms and remaining shrimps into the lake. That made Roger and me happy because the bait smelled bad, and we didn't want to ride in the car with it. When we put the fishing equipment in the trunk of the car, we noticed that Dad had brought our BB guns and a box of BBs, so we spent an hour shooting at Coke cans from different distances. Roger and I tried to see who could hit the middle of the letter "o" in the word Coke.

When we got back to Edcouch, Mom couldn't believe we were home so early.

"Well, did you catch any fish?" Mom asked, hoping we hadn't because she didn't like fish either.

"No, our dumb bait kept falling off," Roger said.

"Yeah, besides, we don't like fish anyway," I said. Dad went straight to the TV to watch the Cowboys play, and Roger and I ran down to our friend's house to show him our new fishing poles.

Calves Never Forget

Buddy Forester stands by the iron gate, waiting for the cows. He feels the rust coming off the iron bars on his hand as he slowly kicks at the ground beneath his boots. The low afternoon sun warms his face as the chilly November air slips under his bluejeans jacket.

He watches Juan and Paco rounding up the cattle across the muddy pasture. The shouts of the men crack the cool air as the cattle move slowly towards Buddy. Off to the side of the corral Old Man Forester's Chevrolet truck comes to a slow stop and he steps out, standing tall as if to say, I own this damn place. He does, but then he always looks as if he owns things, wherever he is.

Old Man Forester's strong frame moves with confidence across his land. His fifty-six-year-old, blue eyes are fixed on Buddy as he adjusts his cap.

"Now, Buddy, when Juan and Paco bring them cows down, don't let those calves get 'round you. Make sure they go in the corral. I don't wanna chase the damn things all over the county." Buddy nods. He knows what to do. He's seen it a dozen times and been through it before. But Old Man Forester likes to give out orders.

"And remember, lock the gate once we got'em in the corral."

"All right, Jack," Buddy says.

Buddy calls him Jack because he can. Almost everybody else calls him Mr. Forester. When people in town introduce Buddy to someone, they say, "This is John Forester's son," which prompts the person to say, "Oh." Those who call Old Man Forester Jack are the other farmers and ranchers. In the morning they all get together at Belva's Fine Diner for coffee. They talk and stand around as if they owned the damn town, and they do.

Old man Forester looks over at Juan and Paco. "Well, c'mon. We haven't got all damn day!"

Juan and Paco start shouting and whistling at the cows.

"Pinches vacas. ¡Ale! Vámonos. ¡Ale! ¿Qué esperan?"

The cows quicken their pace to an awkward trot, forcing steam out of their nostrils as they head towards Buddy. Juan, the joker of the two, yells out at Buddy.

"¡Oye Beto! ¡Ahí se van! "

Buddy grins. Old Man Forester adjusts his cap and frowns. He doesn't like it when Juan calls his son Beto. That's why Forester calls him Buddy, so no one will call him Beto. Buddy doesn't mind, though. After all, it's his name, Alberto.

Alberto Francisco Cuellar is Buddy's birth name. Then he became Alberto Francisco Forester, but Old

Man Forester calls him Buddy, and so does everybody else.

The cows now make their way towards the corral, with their calves running right next to them. Buddy starts to shout and wave his arms to keep them from going around the corral. Juan, Paco, and Old Man Forester surround the cows, shouting and waving. The cattle run into the corral without a hitch. Buddy locks the gate. Now begins the part Buddy hates, the separating of the cows from their calves.

"All right, Juan, Paco, let's go. We haven't got all damn day," Forester says.

Juan and Paco jump into the corral with the nervous cattle. Paco stands by the iron gate, and Juan begins to shout and wave his arms. The cows and their calves run towards the open gate, but Paco lets only the cows out. Juan runs like a dog chasing the cows. He hops to and fro. Juan's wiry, quick body together with his whistling and shouting finally do the job. Only the scared, confused calves remain in the corral.

The cows don't run out to the pasture. Instead, they stand by the iron bars of the corral, wailing. "Shut up, you damn cows!" Old Man Forester yells. The cows keep on wailing. One of the few things he can't control, the cattle making "all that damn racket." The calves, too, start to cry. Buddy hates hearing the cries of the calves. To him, they sound like children crying. Screaming for their mothers.

It was in Weslaco, Texas, in a Piggly Wiggly store, years ago when Old Man Forester and Buddy came across a small Mexican boy crying by the dairy products.

It was the first time Buddy saw the compassionate side of Old Man Forester. The old man carried the sobbing boy to the front of the store, where the manager took over. Buddy remembers asking the old man if it was safe to just leave the small boy with the manager: "Shouldn't we wait for his mother?" The old man said that if the mother wanted her son she'd come looking for him.

Old Man Forester shouts out orders. Juan and Paco respond to the commands. The calves are herded onto a ramp that leads into a trailer. Thirty calves are packed tight in the trailer, still crying out.

Juan and Paco climb into the truck and start down the dirt road leading to the front gate. The starting jolt of the truck knocks the calves off balance, slamming them into each other. Slowly the truck drives away and the cows follow behind crying louder. Once the truck is out the front gate, the cows stop because they can't cross the cattle guard.

Buddy watches the truck turn slowly onto the farm road and disappear behind the trees. The cows stand in a group crying out. Buddy adjusts his cap and looks at Old Man Forester.

"How long will those cows cry like that?"

"A couple of hours or so. Then they'll forget they ever had a calf."

Buddy looks out over the pasture at the cows and wonders if cows really do forget.

Cutting Away

It was a slow Thursday afternoon at the Cut Ends hair salon. Even the parking lot of the shopping center had many open spots. Cindy swept the floor, while Raúl cleaned the mirrors.

Raúl wiped across his reflection, moving the barber tools and instruments on the shelf away from the mirror. He thought to himself of the many things it took just to cut someone's hair: hairspray, assorted brushes and combs, electric razors, scissors, and damn noisy blow dryers.

Cindy swept the black hair into small piles and used the dustpan to pick it up. She said nothing while she swept. Only the sound of the gliding broom, the squeaking of the mirrors being rubbed with paper towels, and the pumping of the window cleaner bottle could be heard.

These moments of silence bothered Raúl. He preferred the sounds of voices to those of brooms and spray bottles. He was now moving Cindy's things, and when he picked up the photograph of her daughter, he knew he had a topic.

"Isn't she just precious?" he asked.

Cindy looked up. "She looks just like her mother," she said with a smile.

Raúl put down the photo and began to wipe his reflection again.

"Has that no-good ex-husband of yours paid his child support this month?" he asked.

Cindy rolled her eyes. "Hell, no! He says he can only give me half because he had to buy new tires for his damn truck. And I'll bet you all the money in the world that he bought the most expensive ones he could find," she said. "You know how he is. Only the best for him, but shit for everybody else. And I'm the one who helped him buy that stupid truck. Walking around like John Travolta in that stupid movie." Cindy stopped to think of the name of the film. "What was the name of that stupid movie? *City Slickers?* No, no, that wasn't it."

Raúl looked at her and put his hands on his hips. "It was *Urban Cowboy*, you silly girl. And, honey, your ex doesn't look anything like John Travolta, but he does look like Billy Crystal, since he's losing his hair and everything."

Cindy laughed and knelt down to pick up the pile of hair she had made. As she began to do so, the front glass door opened, and the hot Valley breeze scattered the pile across the floor. A man walked in, wearing a nice, white shirt and a tie in a bright flowery print. Cindy gave the man a small smile. She would have given him a better smile if he hadn't caused the pile of hair to blow across the tiles.

Raúl noticed the man's clothes and saw that Cindy wasn't in the best position to offer the man a haircut.

"Good afternoon," Raúl said. "Do you need a haircut today?"

The man smiled and said yes, he needed a little off the top and sides. Raúl led him to the back of the salon, "Right this way so I can shampoo your hair." As Raúl walked away, he raised his eyebrows and grinned at Cindy. She smiled back.

Cindy picked up the rest of the hair and put the broom and dustpan away. She was thumbing through one of the magazines when she saw a black Lexus park in front of the salon. It was glossy black with lightly tinted windows. She could see that the driver was a woman with dark, shoulder-length hair. The woman opened the car door and put her foot down on the pavement. She wore black, low-heeled pumps, and her tanned legs seemed to have a nice shape. Cindy wondered what the rest of her looked like.

Raúl walked back in with the man, and Cindy turned to acknowledge them. When she turned back to the window, the woman was walking up to the glass door. She wore a black dress dotted with little, white flowers.

When she walked in, Cindy gave her a friendly "good afternoon" and a nice smile. "Do you need a haircut today or maybe a manicure?" The woman looked more like a young college girl than a woman who would be driving a Lexus. The woman smiled and lightly pulled at the ends of her hair. "I just need a trim."

"Well, come this way so I can shampoo your hair." Cindy began walking but was stopped by the woman's question.

"This won't take long, will it? It's just that I have to be somewhere at six."

Cindy looked up at the clock and saw that it was a quarter to five. "No, it shouldn't take long. I promise I'll have you out in an hour."

The woman followed Cindy into the room, where three white chairs lined up before three black shampoo sinks. Cindy guided the woman into one of the chairs and turned on the water, letting it flow down her hand and rush between her fingers. Cindy gently held the woman's head bent over the contoured sink.

She noticed that the woman had young skin. Smooth skin, without any visible lines, and her hands were tanned the same shade as her ankles and neck.

"Is the water too hot? Does it feel okay?" Cindy asked.

"No, it feels good. I love the way the warm water feels, you know, running over the scalp and everything," the woman replied with her eyes closed.

"Yeah, me too. Sometimes I get Raúl, the other hairdresser, to shampoo my hair just because it's so relaxing."

"That must be great to have someone to shampoo your hair whenever you feel like it," the woman said.

"Yeah, it's great."

Cindy could feel good vibes from this customer. She seemed to be a sweet girl. She put a little extra rub on the girl's scalp and saw her lips curve into a peaceful smile.

She rinsed off the shampoo and began to apply the hair conditioner.

"I'm almost finished, just a couple more minutes."

"Don't worry. Take your time," the woman said.

Cindy smiled as she rubbed. "Well, I just don't want you to be late wherever it is you have to be at six."

"Oh yeah, I'm so relaxed that I almost forgot about that," she said. "In fact, I'm not sure where the place is that I'm supposed to meet this guy for drinks."

Cindy began to rinse her hair. "Oh, you're not from McAllen?"

"No, I'm from Harlingen and I rarely come into McAllen," she said. "I usually go to Brownsville."

Cindy lifted the woman's head out of the shampoo sink. "Well, don't worry. Just tell me the name of the place and I'll tell you where it is. I've been everywhere in this town." Cindy handed her a towel.

The woman started to dry her hair. "Great, for some reason I always get turned around when I come to McAllen."

Cindy let out a chuckle. "Whenever I go to Harlingen, I get turned around. So I guess we have one thing in common and we also like shampoos." Both women laughed. The woman followed Cindy back into the room where the salon chairs were. She sat down, and Cindy put a thin, white plastic cover around her and the chair. She took a comb off the shelf behind her and began to comb back the woman's wet hair.

"So what's the name of the place?"

"He said it was in the Holiday Inn off the 183 Expressway, but I'm not sure how to get there," she said.

Cindy kept combing the woman's hair. "Yeah, that's where MUT's is."

"Muts?"

"Yeah, it's short for the Meet You There lounge; it's a nice bar, and they have a dance floor and play pretty good country music, too."

The woman nodded her head. "Oh, no wonder he wanted to go there."

"What?" Cindy said as she put the comb down and picked up a pair of scissors.

"He likes country music."

"Oh. About how much do you want me to cut off?" Cindy looked at the woman's reflection in the mirror. The woman looked at Cindy holding some of her hair lightly between her fingers.

"Is this much okay?" Cindy asked.

"Yeah, just a little bit. You know, the split ends."

Cindy began taking small cuts. "So this guy likes to dance to country music. Is he a good dancer?"

"Yeah, well, I met him at the South Dallas nightclub here in McAllen."

"Ah, so this is kinda like a date, huh?"

The woman smiled shyly. "Yeah, sort of."

"Well, since you drove all the way from Harlingen just to see him, he at least is cute, right?" Cindy raised her brow. "Because I can't see a pretty girl like you going out with just any ol' guy."

At that point Raúl, who was cutting the man's hair, spoke.

"Well, even if he is cute, you better make him buy you dinner and drinks."

The women laughed, and the man whose hair was being cut said, "And if he doesn't, make him give you gas money."

"Really," Raúl added.

"Yeah," Cindy said.

Raúl went back to cutting the man's hair, and Cindy continued to snip at the woman's hair.

"So he's cute and a good dancer," Cindy said. "Be careful. They are the ones to watch out for. Is he one of those cowboy types, you know, the ones who drive trucks and everything?"

"Yeah, he drives a big, black truck with one of those crazy stickers, you know, the kind that says 'Let's Rodeo' or 'Go Rodeo' or something like that."

Cindy looked over at Raúl, whose face looked worried.

"Raúl, do you know any good-looking guys who drive big, black trucks?"

Raúl paused for a second. "No, but I know the guy who drives the garbage truck down my street, and he looks like Billy Crystal."

The woman in the chair laughed a bit. "Well, this guy says he works for the city, and I don't think he drives a garbage truck, but he kinda does look like Billy Crystal."

Cindy's mind flashed back to the time when she had found a pair of torn panty hose and one earring in her ex-husband's truck. He said that he had lent his truck to a friend and that it wasn't him, but she knew he was lying. She could always tell when a man was lying. They all lied the same way.

She had been so mad that she had taken a screwdriver out of his tool chest and carved out the words "Yo Soy Puto" on the tailgate of his truck. She also scratched the word "Asshole" on the sides. He had to drive around for a week before he could get his truck repainted. And now she was cutting the hair of a possible—what he would call—"a notch in my belt."

Cindy's eyes focused back on the woman's black hair. "What could this nice girl see in that asshole?" she thought to herself. "She probably fell for all his sweet bullshit lines."

"So is this guy nice?" Cindy asked.

"Yeah, he seems to be pretty nice and all," the woman answered. "His truck is four-wheel drive and he wants to take me off-roading. Which sounds pretty crazy, but he looks like he likes to have that kind of crazy fun, you know?"

Cindy held some hair in her hand and stopped cutting, "Now, how much did say you wanted me to cut off? Just a little, right?"

"Yeah, just a little."

Raúl gave the man his change for the haircut and walked over to Cindy and the woman.

"Honey, if you like I'll finish her hair so you can go pick up your little girl," Raúl said.

The woman looked at the photograph of the little girl, "Oh, is that your daughter?"

Cindy took the frame in her hand and nodded. "Yeah, she's my baby."

"She's so cute. How old is she?"

Cindy handed the woman the photograph. "She's two."

The woman studied the photograph for a few seconds. "She looks just like you."

Cindy nodded. "Yeah, that's what people say, but I think she has her father's eyes. They're the kind of eyes people say they feel they can trust."

"Oh," the woman said and handed the photograph back to Cindy.

"I'll be happy to finish her hair so you can pick her up from your mother's house," Raúl said with a smile.

Cindy put her hands on her hips and raised her brow. "Raúl, I'm almost finished. Besides, I know what kind of hair good-looking, dancing cowboys like, and you don't!"

Raúl put his hands on his hips. "Oh yes, I do, and I know what kind of hair they like on men, too!"

Cindy laughed and the woman in the chair chuckled.

"No, but really. If you want me to, I'll be happy to do her hair," Raúl said.

The woman in the chair spoke. "I don't mind. If you need to pick up your daughter, it's okay with me if he does my hair."

Cindy couldn't help liking the sweet girl. "No, honey, I want to do your hair. My daughter is with my mother so she's fine."

Raúl shrugged his shoulders and went about sweeping the floor and tidying up the salon.

Cindy continued with her job and thought how dumb it was to get a little mad just because this woman was go ing out with her ex. They had been divorced for over a year now, and she couldn't blame her for going out with him. After all, he could be very charming when he wanted to be. At their wedding he had been charming and romantic.

Cindy combed and clipped, moving the hair back and forth, making sure the lines were straight. The woman sat still and began talking about how much McAllen had grown. Cindy gave standard answers, focusing on the woman's hair.

She put gel in the woman's hair and used the blow dryer to shape it. All those years of being in love . . . I should just let it go, Cindy thought to herself. She brushed the hair some more and then teased it lightly.

"I'm going to use a little bit of hairspray; is that okay with you?" Cindy asked.

"Yeah, whatever you think is fine with me."

Cindy sprayed and combed some more, then stood back to look at the woman's hair. The woman looked in the mirror and was surprised to see how good she looked. She turned her head to the right and left, keeping her eyes on her reflection. Raúl came in from the shampoo room and walked over to Cindy and the customer.

"Honey, you look great," Raúl said.

The woman looked at Raúl's reflection. "It does look good, doesn't it?"

"Oh yeah, honey."

Cindy nodded her head slightly. "You like it?"

"Yes, I do. You did a great job," the woman said.

"Yeah, she looks great," Raúl said.

Cindy said nothing for a couple of seconds. "I'm glad you like it. I just wanted you to look good for your date."

"Well, even if he doesn't like it, I know I do," the woman said.

The woman paid for the haircut, and Cindy drew a map for her.

"Here's a map so you won't get lost, and you still have fifteen minutes to get there."

"Thanks for everything," the woman said. "And by the way, what's your name?"

Cindy stood still for a second and then put out her hand. "I'm Sandra."

The woman shook her hand. "I'm Gracie. When I'm back in town I'll try to stop by so you can do my hair again, and most of all, shampoo me. Thanks."

Cindy watched the woman get into her car. Before she drove off, she waved good-bye and Cindy waved back. Raúl walked up behind Cindy and stood next to her as the woman drove off.

"Are you all right?" Raúl asked.

Cindy nodded.

"You did a great job on her hair, you know," Raúl said. "I was kinda afraid you were going to chop it all off."

"I thought about it, but he's not worth anything anymore."

Raúl put his arm around her, and they both looked out at the empty parking lot. He turned his head to look at her. "Why don't we close early today?"

Cindy kept looking out at the parking lot. She slowly turned to look at him.

"Yeah . . . it's time to close."

Building a Mountain

Joe watches the giant crane lift the concrete support beams across the unfinished highway. It swings the beam in one smooth, graceful move, as if the beam were made of crystal. He sits in his ten-wheeler wondering how he could learn to operate that crane. The guy inside makes more money than he does, and he doesn't get dirty. He just sits and swings this way and that, all day long.

He hears the high-pitched whistle telling him that his truck is filled with dirt. Dust surrounds his truck and blows into his cab, adding to the many layers on his brown skin. Joe puts the truck in gear and drives up the big hill of rocks and dirt. He dumps his load and goes back down the hill for another. For the past six months, from six-thirty in the morning to four-thirty in the afternoon, this has been Joe's job. Dumping dirt.

On his way home at the end of the day he stops to get a quart of whatever is on sale, so long as it's cold. As he steps out of his Chevrolet truck, he slaps some dust out of his blue jeans and readjusts the fit. They're loose jeans and a little too long but comfortable.

He likes the feel of the air-conditioned wind rushing out when he opens the glass doors of the store. If only his house were this cool. It must be nice to work inside an air-conditioned building all day long, he thinks to himself.

Joe feels the bottles of beer to see which is the coldest; usually the ones in the back row are. Walking down the aisle, he stops at the candy rack. He forgets what kind of candy bars his children like, so he grabs three Hershey chocolate bars. That should make them happy, he thinks to himself.

At home Joe is greeted by the wide smiles of his children. They surround him because they know that, as always, he has something for each of them. He lifts the youngest up in the air and gives her a kiss. Her four-year-old body rests on his chest as he walks through the house.

"¿Dónde está tu mamá?" He asks his oldest. His seven-year-old son tells him she's in the kitchen making something to eat.

From the kitchen, his wife speaks so all the kids can hear.

"Don't eat any candy until you eat your dinner."

Joe looks at his children. "¿Oyeron?" His kids nod with small grins.

Joe's wife looks into the pot of beans and the pan of rice cooking on the stove. Her black hair is in a tight bun, and beads of sweat lightly cover her forehead. She wipes her hands on her apron and calls out that it's time to turn off the TV and come to the table. She looks at her husband holding their daughter.

"And you, at least wash your hands," she says in the same tone she uses with the children.

She sets the plates of rice, beans, and carne guisada on the small table. She puts the tortillas wrapped in a dish towel in the center of the table. Joe comes out of the bathroom, drying his hands on his jeans, and sits at the table ready to eat. With clean hands, Joe reaches for the tortillas, but his wife clears her voice, "Joe, first we give thanks. Then we eat."

Joe smiles and the children giggle. They all put their hands together and Joe's wife begins saying grace.

"Thank you, Lord, for this meal we are about to receive and the wonderful family you have given us. I pray that you watch over our family, and that Joe gets a chance to be a crane operator. Thank you, Lord. For thine is the kingdom, and the power, and the glory, forever and ever. Amen."

All the family says amen, and Joe again goes for the tortillas.

His wife asks how his day was.

Joe nods. "It was good. I carried forty loads."

"Is that a lot, Daddy?" his oldest asks.

"Yeah, m'hijo. Yesterday, I only carried thirty-six loads so that's . . . how many more? You tell me, m'hijo."

"Four!" his middle son exclaims with a smile.

"That's right, René." He looks at his oldest son. "Your little brother is learning pretty fast, eh, Román?" Román agrees and René smiles wider. Joe looks over at his wife, who is also smiling, and he can tell what she is going to ask.

"Honey, did you talk to your boss today about being a crane operator?"

"We were very busy today and I didn't have time to ask him," he answers as he puts another mouthful of food in his mouth. "Mañana, ¿bueno?"

"You told me you would ask him today, Joe."

"Sí, honey, I was going to, but he was busy and I was busy."

His wife looks down at her plate and moves the beans with her fork.

"Joe, you quit your last job because you were tired of being a truck driver, remember? And now you're doing the same thing," she says in a patient tone, trying not to be the one who will later be blamed for starting an argument.

"Honey, this is different. I am not just hauling vegetables or fruit. I'm part of a team of workers building something. Something that later I can tell my children, 'I helped build that highway,'" he says.

The children sit and listen to their father and try to visualize the highway.

"Sí, Joe, but . . . if you were a crane operator you could say that, but all you're doing is making a big pile of dirt."

Joe raises his voice. "That's not just a big pile of dirt. That's going to be an on-ramp for cars."

"Joe, it's still a big pile of dirt and you could do more. You could be a crane operator or one of those guys on top of the expressway. You know the guys who tell the crane guy where to put things down," she says. "You can do more, honey—that's why I want you to be a crane operator."

Joe says nothing. He just puts another mouthful of beans in his mouth and reaches over to ruffle his daughter's hair. She smiles at her father. He looks across the table at his wife.

"Mira, when I get a chance, I'll talk to the boss and see what he says, ¿bueno?"

"When?"

"Honey, right now I like what I'm doing. It's not so bad, and I'm getting more money than I did when I worked for the produce company, okay?" He says. "It's a good job, and when the time comes I'll ask the boss. Now let me eat. I don't want to talk about it anymore."

His wife knows when to quit and says nothing more. The next morning Joe drives to work thinking about that big pile of dirt. He knows the job doesn't offer anything new. Instead of vegetables and fruit, it's dirt, but, still, he likes this better, he thinks to himself.

As he approaches the work site, the first thing he can see is the big pile of dirt. It's big. He has never really thought about it, but it is huge. He parks his truck and says "good morning" to the workmen and walks over to the pile. He stops at the base and begins walking around it, keeping his eyes on the peak.

The morning sun bathes the pile in a soft, orange light. It looks like the pyramids he's seen in books and on TV. As he goes around it, he can see its dark shadow extending beyond the unfinished highway and slowly creeping off the office building across the finished highway. This isn't a pile of dirt, he thinks to himself.

That day Joe hauls forty-five loads of dirt. Back and forth he drives as fast as he can, trying to see if he can make it higher. At lunchtime, he drives his truck to the top and tries to figure out how tall his pile of dirt is. He can see over the double-overpass expressway across the way, but how high off the ground is the highest overpass? Sixty or seventy feet at the most, he thinks, but his pile has to be at least seventy, maybe eighty or ninety, feet high. He just doesn't know. He thinks about asking the engineer, Debbie Ruiz, because she is a lot nicer than the men and she's Mexican American.

As he loads and unloads dirt, he keeps an eye out for Ms. Ruiz. Close to four o'clock, he sees her walk into the air-conditioned main trailer, and he tells one of the men he is taking a five-minute break.

On entering the trailer, he sees her immediately. He approaches her and asks her if she can tell him how high the pile of dirt is. Ms. Ruiz asks why and he tells her he is the one who hauls the dirt up and down all day, and he just wants to know so he can tell his kids. Ms. Ruiz agrees and goes outside with Joe to take a look at the pile.

She takes out some instruments Joe has seen others use. She looks through them and writes down some numbers and then takes out her calculator. After a minute or so, she comes up with the height.

"Now this is just an estimate, but it's pretty close. The pile of dirt is about 120 feet high," she says. "It might be a little higher, and by the time you're done it should be over 140 feet high, maybe even 150."

"That high?"

"Well, it has to be, because this will be where we put the on-ramp that will go over those two expressways," she continues. "So, that's about eleven or twelve stories high."

"Eleven or twelve stories," he repeats.

"Yeah, what you're building is more of a mountain than a pile."

That evening at the dinner table Joe tells his family what the engineer has said about the pile of dirt. When he tells his kids how tall the pile of dirt is, they are amazed.

"As tall as a twelve-story building," Román exclaims. "Wow, Daddy, that's real tall."

"Is that real high?" René asks.

"Yeah, René, it's like stacking twelve of our houses on top of each other," Román says. "That's how high Daddy's pile of dirt is."

Joe is happy that the kids were getting a kick out of it.

"Can we see it, Daddy?" René asks.

"Yeah, Daddy, I'd like to get on top of it and see everything," Román adds.

"Sure, tomorrow I'll take all three of you to see it," Joe says proudly. "And we'll climb to the top so you can see how high it is."

The children smile and look happy about getting to see their father's mountain. Joe's wife looks happy, too.

"You got to talk to one of the engineers?" She asked.

"Yeah, Debbie Ruiz, she's from Houston and is real nice," Joe says still smiling.

"Well, why didn't you ask her about training to be a crane guy," she asks. "I mean, maybe she can put in a good word for you or something."

"Honey, she's not in charge of hiring people. She is just one of the engineers on the project," Joe says.

"Sí, honey, but maybe she knows some people who could tell you how to be a crane guy. You should at least ask," she continues. "I mean, if you can ask an engineer about how tall your pile of dirt is, then you can ask them about working on the crane."

Joe says nothing. He looks at his plate of food and thinks only of placating her.

"You're right. Monday I'll ask one of them, or I'll ask Debbie Ruiz about being a crane operator, okay?" With that his wife says no more, and the table becomes quiet.

The next day Joe shows his kids the mountain of dirt he has been building. When he tells them where he is taking them, they become excited and ask if he is going to take them to the top. "Sure," he says proudly. "We'll go to the very top."

He carries his daughter in his arms as they begin the climb up the giant pile. His sons pick up rocks as they walk, throwing them in every direction. Once at the top, the kids are surprised how high up they are.

"This is really high, Daddy," Román says. "It's like being on top of a building or something."

Joe puts his daughter down, and each of them begin picking up rocks and throwing them. Cars dash along the finished expressway nearby. Joe shows them the truck he drives, and they are impressed because the truck is made of metal, instead of wood like the truck he drove for the produce company. Joe and the kids are having fun, and the kids comment every so often, "You made this mountain, Daddy?" Joe tells them, "Sure did, and I'm not even finished yet."

When they get home, the kids waste no time telling their mother about the mountain of dirt. They go on about how "you can see everything from up there." Their mother smiles and asks if the crane is taller than Daddy's mountain. Román and René says "No way, Mom. This mountain is big." Joe can see that his wife is not impressed by the kids' description.

"Honey, you want to go for a ride or something?" He asks. "We can have your sister watch the kids."

She looks at him and can sense he wants some time alone with her. "Si quieres," she says.

They go out for a drink and some food at a nearby Mexican restaurant. They eat, drink, and talk. They talk about the children and how lucky they are to have such smart kids. After he downs a couple of beers and she drinks a margarita, they both begin to have that look about them. The look that came before their children and made them grin a certain way. Joe feels good.

On the way home Joe decides to show her the mountain. It is such a wonderful night, and the cool, soft breeze will feel even better from up high. She doesn't ask about their destination; it feels good not knowing where she is going.

Joe pulls into the construction site as if he is pulling into his driveway at home. It is familiar to him, it feels right.

"What are we doing here, Joe?" She asks.

"I want to show you something," he says. "You might like it."

They walk over to the mountain holding hands, and she says nothing as they walk. Joe looks at her and says, "We're going up this mountain of dirt. You'll see how cool it is when we reach the top." Again she says nothing and holds his hand as he leads the way.

At the top a cool breeze moves her black hair in a waving motion, and their clothes fold to the shaping wind. He holds her hand as they look out over the expressway and the unfinished roads. It is high, she thinks to herself. Joe lets go of her hand and walks a few steps away.

"I made this, baby. It took me months, but I built this mountain and I'm not finished yet," he says. "What do you think? It's high, eh?"

She looks around. "Yeah, it's high, but it's still just a pile of dirt, Joe."

"What do you mean? This is not just a pile of dirt. This pile is over eleven stories high; it's the highest thing around." He points at the surroundings. "Look around you. Nothing is higher except the downtown buildings. I built this."

She stood looking at him. "Joe, this is a pile of dirt, Joe. ¡Es todo y nada más!"

With that she begins walking down the mountain.

He watches her walking away and looks around. He can see everything. So high up and away from the ground. He looks over at her again and shouts "Ah sí, why don't you tell God that the Earth is nothing but a big ball of dirt!"

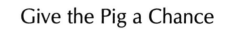
Give the Pig a Chance

Freddy could feel his legs falling asleep as he sat on the toilet, but the article he was reading in his favorite tabloid about the strange "batchild" found somewhere in the Ozark Mountains was getting good. He wiggled his toes to help the blood circulate through his thick legs and shifted his weight from side to side, making the toilet seat slide as he swayed.

He could hear heavy footsteps on the wooden floors coming down the short hall. The heavy steps stopped in front of the restroom door.

"Freddy! Freddy!" His cousin Carlos shouted through the door.

Freddy frowned, took his eyes away from the "bat-child" story, and looked at the locked door.

"What!"

"That damn hog of yours is in my restroom!" Carlos shouted as he pointed down the hall. "I already told you that if he did that again I'd make chorizo out of him."

"And I told you to keep your restroom door closed and Arnold won't go in there!" Freddy shouted back.

"Yeah, well, why don't you make that damn pig of yours go outside to use the restroom?"

"Because he's house-trained, that's why!" Freddy yelled. "If you want, I'll train him to take a shit on your bed."

Carlos stormed down the hall and out the back screen door. Freddy listened to the heavy feet stomp across the floor and heard the back door open and slam. He quickly took some toilet paper and wiped himself and felt the thousands of needles pricking his legs as his veins filled with blood. He raised himself from the toilet and looked out the bathroom window and saw Carlos relieving himself by the mesquite tree.

"Who's the pig now?" Freddy shouted through the half-opened window and laughed to himself.

Carlos looked over his shoulder at the bathroom window and then looked back again at the plowed dirt fields. He didn't know how much more he could take, but he knew that within a couple of days he would be promoted to manager of the Pollo Palace, and then he could move out. He was qualified for the job, having been a manager of the Dairy Queen back in Three Rivers, Texas, for the past five years. Hell, if I could run that busy Dairy Queen, I sure as hell can run the Pollo Palace in little Edcouch, he thought to himself.

It had been eight months since he left Three Rivers, and his wife was still not answering his letters or his phone calls. He missed his daughter and son, but he knew better than to go near them, and besides his in-laws and six brothers-in-law had made a few promises that they were planning to see come true should he try to go back, and then there was the whole Gunter family to deal with.

Carlos looked down at his penis as he urinated. "This is all you're good for from now on. You can only come out to piss and that's it," he said.

As he walked back to the house he could hear eggs frying and his tía Bebe talking to Arnold. She talked more to Arnold than she talked to anybody else. Tía Bebe poured him a cup of coffee as he sat down at the kitchen table. She was the only one who would take him in after everything had gone to hell in Three Rivers. His mother and tía Bebe were sisters, and though tía Bebe may have had her opinion on what Carlos had done, she never brought up the subject.

Arnold, the family pet, a white potbellied pig, walked underneath the table and sniffed Carlos's work shoes. They always smelled like chicken and Arnold liked to lick them. Carlos had learned to ignore the pig's small pleasures—licking shoes, sleeping on his bed, and using the toilet in the house.

Freddy came in, and Carlos could see that he was in the mood for an argument.

"So how's the assistant manager of PP this morning?"

Carlos said nothing and kept drinking his coffee. Tía Bebe placed a plate of scrambled eggs and tortillas on the table in front of Carlos.

"Gracias, tía," he said.

"¿Quieres más café?" she asked.

Carlos said yes and she poured some in his cup and gave Freddy a cup, too. Carlos continued eating but could feel Freddy's eyes burning on him. Tía Bebe set down a plate for Freddy. "Ten, m'hijo," she said. Freddy looked up. "Thanks, Mom," he replied.

Both men were quiet for a moment and tía Bebe left the kitchen to go watch TV.

"I spoke to Cousin Mimi yesterday," Freddy said.

Carlos could feel his body tense but said nothing.

"She told me why Lisa kicked you out."

Carlos looked across the table and again had no comment. Freddy smirked and raised his brow.

"She said that you got a little, white teenage girl who worked for you pregnant, then . . . "

"Shut up, Freddy."

"You drove her to San Antonio so she could have an abortion," Freddy continued.

Carlos said nothing and rose to leave the table.

"Imagine that. A thirty-seven-year-old man fucking a teenage girl," Freddy said. "Man, you're disgusting."

"At least I'm not a thirty-four-year-old man fucking a pig like you, pervert."

"You're the pervert!" Freddy shouted. "What's next, some girl at the Pollo Palace?"

Carlos left the house and tried to calm his anger as he drove. He got to the Pollo Palace and sat at one of the gold-colored tables, watching the slow traffic pass by. In twenty minutes, two employees would show up. He felt like talking to someone who could understand, but he didn't even understand himself how everything had gotten so screwed up. One year ago he was doing fine, opening the Dairy Queen at ten and picking up his kids at three-thirty from school and then back to DQ for chocolate dip cones and burger busters. It was a great life, and now he was in a hole so deep he couldn't see a way out.

The rest of the day Carlos worked on automatic. He let the work eat his thoughts as he'd been doing for the past eight months, the busier the better. The only time his memory screamed was when he saw a pregnant woman or a little boy or girl. He had taken no days off since starting and was earning enough to send his family something every two weeks. Every day he was in by nine and worked until midnight—it was the perfect schedule. By the time he got home he was too tired to think, and in the morning he was too tired to recall any of his dreams.

At closing time he let the employees take home leftovers. They would box chicken and fries for themselves, and Carlos would take a small bucket home for Freddy and his pig. He would pack breasts of chicken and fries, which Freddy liked best, and take him a large diet soda. But this particular night all he packed was wings and no fries. Freddy hated wings.

On the drive home he felt like having a beer, but tomorrow was going to be an important day. Mr. Wilson, the owner of the Pollo Palace chain, was coming to Edcouch to tell Carlos personally whether or not he had gotten the promotion. It was a big day, and if he got the promotion, it would be a chance to do something right.

Turning into the driveway, he saw the bluish light from the TV and knew Freddy was waiting for some fried chicken. Carlos parked the car and sat for a moment listening to the engine ticking as it cooled. His body was tired and his right leg trembled and jerked; it just didn't want to stop. His body wouldn't let him rest.

Getting out of the car, he struggled carrying the bucket of chicken and the large soda. As he walked behind the car, his leg caught the end of the bumper and he fell. His knees hit the gravel driveway as the soda and bucket of chicken hit the ground.

Carlos stayed on his knees for a few seconds. He couldn't feel his knees bleeding: his body was too tired to register minor pain. He got up and picked up the empty soda cup. He noticed the lid of the bucket was half off, and he saw the silhouettes of a few chicken wings on the ground. He closed the lid and staggered to the door.

Arnold stood by the door waiting. He knew the door would swing open and then he could run out by squeezing through between Carlos's legs and the door.

As Carlos opened the door, Freddy yelled, "Arnold! Arnold, don't you dare!"

But Arnold squirmed through and ran out.

"Shit, man! I told you not to let Arnold out!" Freddy shouted at Carlos.

Carlos said nothing and set the bucket down and went into the kitchen. Freddy got up, walked to the table, and picked up the empty cup. He looked in it and then began digging through the bucket.

"Hey, man, there's nothing in here but wings," he said. "What the hell?"

Carlos ignored Freddy and poured himself a glass of water.

"Hey, I'm talking to you," Freddy said. "There's nothing but wings in here. I told you that I hate wings, and where's my coke, man?"

Carlos took a drink and looked over at Freddy and said nothing.

Freddy glared at Carlos. "Hey, I'm . . . ," he began.

"Go to hell, Freddy. You're so damn fat, why the hell should I care what you put in your fat fucking mouth," Carlos said in an angry voice.

"Hey, man, I'm not the one who's fat. You're the one who's fat," Freddy yelled.

"Look in the mirror, Freddy. You eat more than that damn pig of yours," Carlos said. "Every night stuffing that fat fucking mouth like a pig."

"Nah, man. You're fat. I've always been like this, so this is my natural body weight," Freddy said. "You were always skinny and now you're fat. Fat because all you do is go around screwing little girls."

Freddy kept on saying things. Things about how Carlos was at fault for everything and ruined everything he touched. Every day for the past eight months Freddy had some comment, and Carlos just took it because he deserved the abuse. That Catholic guilt was working double time on him, and it was finally getting to him. If he couldn't be forgiven then he would fight the reminders.

Carlos threw the glass into the sink, shattering it, and charged Freddy. Both men crashed into the table, cursing and yelling, and then slammed into the wall, knocking down wall fixtures and the clock. Tía Bebe came out of her bedroom screaming and crying.

"Ay Dios, please stop it," she screamed.

The two men continued swinging as she tried to pull them apart.

"Alfredo, m'hijo, stop it, stop it, please," she begged, tugging at her son's shoulder.

Carlos and Freddy pushed each other apart and Carlos stormed out the door. Freddy moved towards him, with his mother holding on to his arm.

"Come back and fight!" he shouted.

Carlos got in his car, turned on the ignition, and shifted the car into reverse. Through the sound of spinning tires he heard a high-pitched scream. It was the scream a pig makes when it's being castrated, when all its aggression moves through its body and escapes in screeching sounds.

Freddy ran out of the house with his mother close behind, and Carlos jumped out of the car. On the ground screaming and twisting was Freddy's pig, Arnold. Blood gushed out of its head and covered its white hair. The blood looked black in the red glow of the tail lights. Freddy grabbed Arnold and tried to hold him still, but the pig kicked and jerked violently forcing Freddy to let it go. Arnold fell to the ground kicking and twisting. Carlos was horrified at the sight, and tía Bebe clenched and tugged at her nightgown.

They stood still watching Arnold's kicks and jerks come to a slow stop until the only motion was his tail twitching. Carlos closed his eyes and put his face in his hands. Tía Bebe moved closer to Freddy and placed her hand on his shoulder. She said his name a couple of times, almost whispering as if not to wake him, but he didn't move. Freddy's eyes filled with tears as he knelt down beside his pet. Gently he reached out to cradle Arnold in his arms. Carlos knelt down to help him, but Freddy turned his back.

"Get away!" Freddy shouted. "Can't you see you've done enough?"

Carlos held out his hands. "I'm sorry, I didn't . . ."

"Sorry, that's it? You're sorry?" Freddy said. "Well, being sorry is not enough, Carlos."

Freddy walked back into the house, and tía Bebe followed him quietly.

Carlos leaned on his car for a moment and put his head down on the roof and listened to them walk away. He waited until the front door closed and then he got in his car and drove to the closest bar he could find. He sat and drank, thinking of that pig he had killed. It was a perfect pig. It never bothered or bit anyone and it was even house-trained. He thought of how he had killed his marriage; it was perfect, too. Lisa was a wonderful wife and their son and daughter were angels. Carlos took out his wallet and flipped through the photos of his family. How can I make all this right again? he thought to himself. He could feel tears pressing on his eyeballs, but he took a deep breath and got up to order another drink.

The next morning Carlos's body ached. He couldn't blame the alcohol. Every morning he felt the same way, as if someone had beaten him and left him to live another day. He got up and dressed for work. The house was quiet, and he could tell it was because Arnold was missing. He went into the kitchen where tía Bebe was sitting at the table drinking coffee. The wall fixtures were still on the floor and the table was pushed up against the wall from the fight hours before.

Carlos picked up a chair from the floor and sat down at the table with tía Bebe. She sat still and kept her eyes on her coffee. Carlos searched for something to say, but he couldn't sort out his emotions. He wasn't sure what to be sorry about first.

Tía Bebe took a drink and looked up at Carlos.

"Remember when you were a little boy and you broke your Mama Locha's wedding vase?" she asked. Carlos nodded.

"You tried to fix it with glue and tape, but it still wasn't right. If you ran your fingers across it, you could get cut because it wasn't smooth anymore," she said. "So you broke your piggy bank and bought her a new vase. It wasn't the same, but it didn't cut you when you held it. It made your Mama Locha very happy."

At work he tried to take his mind off things by inspecting the kitchen. He wiped here and there and then sat and watched the cars pass by. Morning was the only time of the day when he could sit in silence, and it was these morning minutes that squeezed his heart because he could hear the voices of his family.

Across the street from the Pollo Palace was a vacant lot, and he could imagine his children on the playground. They would swing back and forth on the swing set. Carlos would stay hypnotized deep in his daydream until the first workers arrived, then he would awaken and see a vacant lot again.

Carlos went about his job and his employees went about theirs; he had forgotten that Mr. Wilson was coming. When Mr. Wilson knocked on the glass door, one of the employees told him they didn't open until ten. When Carlos heard the knock, he quickly came out from the back and let the owner in.

Mr. Wilson, a no-nonsense man, got right to the point. "Carlos, congratulations, you're the new manager of Pollo Palace here in Edcouch," he said with a smile. He gave Carlos a white envelope and shook his hand. "There's a little something for you in the envelope. Good luck." With that, Mr. Wilson walked out the glass door and drove away.

Carlos watched the man drive off and was surprised that it was over so quickly. Opening the envelope, he found three crisp one-hundred-dollar bills and a letter. The letter said, "Welcome to the team and don't spend the bonus all in one place."

He paced the floor for a few moments and then told his two workers he was taking the rest of the day off. The two employees looked at each other with surprise, and one said, "Sure, you're the boss."

Carlos drove to McAllen because he knew it had a big mall. It seemed as though he were the only customer in the mall, and he walked around a bit; he had forgotten how big these malls could be. It had everything, even a pet store.

The pet store was jumping with sound and movement from dogs, cats, birds, snakes, hamsters, lizards, ferrets, and one black potbellied pig. Carlos knelt down to pet the small pig. It snorted and wobbled, sticking its nose in his palm.

"Cute pig, huh?" A smiling young woman asked.

"Yeah, these pigs are something else," he said.

"And smart, too," she said. "They say they're smarter than dogs and you can house-train them."

Carlos nodded. "Is this the only one you have?"

"No, we have another one in the back. One of the guys is giving it a bath."

"Oh, what color is it?"

"Black. Just like this one," she said.

"Do you know who would have a white one?" He asked.

"Nobody else in the Valley has potbellied pigs but us," she said, "and right now all we have is two black ones."

"How much is one?"

"Two hundred."

"Two hundred!" Carlos exclaimed.

"Yeah," the woman nodded. "Potbellied pigs aren't cheap, but they make great pets and they're easy to house-train and you can even walk them on a leash, just like a dog."

Carlos put his hands on his hips and thought for a second. "And you're sure nobody else has potbellied pigs in the Valley, not even in Brownsville or Harlingen?"

"We're the only ones," she said with a shrug of her shoulders.

Carlos knelt back down and petted the pig some more. The pig rubbed its face in his hand and snorted.

"Okay, I'll take this one," he said as he stood.

Carlos walked out with the pig in a box and pamphlets on how to care for a potbellied pig. He hoped Freddy would like it and that his gesture would show how sorry he was; this pig could make things better for him, and it would be a chance to set things right.

When he drove up to the house, all the windows were open and he could hear the TV blaring in the living room. He parked the car and walked into the house. Freddy didn't move from his chair and continued watching the screen.

"Freddy," Carlos said. "Freddy, please, Freddy, turn down the TV. I got something to show you." Freddy hit the remote and the screen went black.

"What?" He asked.

"It's out in the car," Carlos said and began walking out.

The two men walked out to the car, and Freddy stood with his arms crossed as Carlos opened the door and reached in to take the pig out of the box. He held the pig in his arms as if he were holding a baby.

"I went and got you a potbellied pig." Carlos smiled hopefully.

Freddy's eyes showed interest, but he didn't move and kept his arms crossed. "You think it's that easy, huh? Just buy him another one, like they're all the same or something."

Carlos held the pig close to his chest and slowly shook his head.

"Well, they're not the same. Arnold was a great pet and you can't just go and replace him with this pig."

"I know, I know this pig is not Arnold, but you can train him and . . ."

Freddy shook his head and kept his arms crossed. Carlos could see that Freddy didn't want to forgive him. He could feel the pulse of the little pig on his chest, and its warm body gave him a strange sense of love. Carlos gently tightened his hold on the pig.

"Freddy, I know, I know I made some terrible mistakes and I'm sorry, but you don't have to forgive me, really, you don't. But I'm really sorry, I, I . . ." Carlos's body was getting weak and he could feel his legs buckling. His voice broke and tears began rolling down his quivering face. He couldn't stop his knees from hitting the ground. "Please, please, just take the pig. I know it's not the same and everything, but if you love it, then it'll be a good pig. I know it will."

Freddy's frown turned into a worried look as he watched his cousin sobbing on his knees. Carlos extended his arms and held the pig up to Freddy, begging him to take the pig.

"Please, please, I'm sorry, I'm so damn sorry about everything, but if you just give this pig a chance, I promise it'll be good and it'll love you with all its heart. Please, please," Carlos said, his voice breaking.

Freddy put out his hands and took the pig with one and with the other rubbed Carlos's back. "Primo, it's going to be all right, it's going to be all right."

Carlos put his sobbing face in his hands. "Please, just give me a chance."